NecRomance

NecRomance

Autumn Equinox

Warning: Depictions of sex and fantasy violence. Excessive vulgar language.

Self-published by the author.

Cover art concept illustrated by Liam Sullivan, Instagram: @sketchysully
Cover art and inner art designed by Ezra Komo, Instagram: @ezrakomo_como
Additional cover art provided by Canva
About the Author photo by Brandon Banks @brandonbanksphotography

Library of Congress Cataloging-in-Publication Data:

Names: Equinox, Autumn / Thompson, Connor (Author)
Title: NecRomance by Autumn Equinox
Other titles: NecRomance
Description: First edition.
Identifiers: Copyright ID# ISBN: 978-1-7367748-6-1 (trade pbk.)
Subject: Fiction – Fantasy. Fiction – LGBTQ. Fiction – Action/Adventure.

First edition:

This book is dedicated to any non-binary/trans folk who wish to see themselves as heroes. The chosen ones, magical and capable of writing their own stories. You are <u>not</u> NPC's.

For Matt & Michael. Two very decent best friends.

1

A Less Than Standard Haunting

The upside to working with the dead was the price people were willing to pay to bring peace to their lost loved ones. A séance came with a bill of $2000. A standard haunting normally yielded a solid $5000, before taxes. Thus, the 28-year-old Romy – a necromancer – was able to make a sustainable living, all the while easing the pain and suffering of both the living and the dead.

On the morning before the summer solstice, they made a house call to a great colonial manor in the upscale Boston suburb of Brookline. A full mile before arriving, they could already sense a great ghastly presence. By the time they reached the door, they felt like they were being pulled into a terrible void of grief and pain.

They pondered charging double.

They knocked. An icy cold wind blew through their dark hair and a gaunt, grey woman in her fifties in an unwashed black dress appeared at the door. The wind brought with it a stench that told Romy that she hadn't bathed in days.

"Hello," she said with an exhausted whisper. "Thank you for coming."

They smiled without showing their teeth. "Hello. I'm Romy."

"Karen."

"Hi, Karen. How are you?"

She looked as if she were going to cry, but her tear ducts had long expired. "Please, come inside."

They did not want to, but they needed to.

An ordinary person might have seen a beautiful house, with chic wallpaper and expensive furniture. But Romy, with their magicked eyes, saw nothing but shadows. All vibrating and radiating with a soul-sucking pain.

"By the Heathen Gods," they said, under their breath as their already pale skin turned almost translucent.

"You can see it? The darkness?"

"How long has this been going on?"

"I have no idea. I haven't slept in so long. I've lost track of the days." She became faint and began to fall.

Romy caught her before she hit the ground. Things were worse than they ever could have imagined. "We need to get you out of here. Right now."

Her body went limp in their arms. "I can't."

They held her up with all their strength. "Yes, you can."

"No. I can't. She won't let me."

"Who?"

"Mother."

The room became colder.

Romy knew they had to make their escape immediately. "I'll take care of her. But first we need to get you out of this house."

The door slammed closed. What felt like a chorus of voices composed of pure hatred whispered in their ear. *"It's better this way."*

Romy should have shivered, but they were used to creepy voices. "Yeah, no." They activated their Hue, draping themself in a brilliant magenta light in the process as they accessed the magic deep within. Raising their hand, they conjured a sigil with their power, enacting a spell designed to distract disembodied entities. *"Momeală cursă."*

The air, once thick with a haze of rage, lightened. While the shadows remained, the intangible presence behind them felt less present.

"What did you do?" Karen weakly asked.

"Tricked them into thinking we were somewhere else," They explained as they opened the door and dragged her outside. "It's hard to keep track of people when you exist outside the confines of time and space."

As soon as they made it to the front lawn, Karen collapsed onto the ground and the door slammed shut behind them.

With a sense of great urgency, Romy pulled out their phone and dialed 9-1-1. "Hello, I have a woman who needs medical attention at Fifty-One Estate Boulevard. Malnourishment. Exhaustion. Hasn't eaten or slept in days. Please, send help." They looked down at her shivering, quivering, skeletal body on the ground, clutching the grass like a blanket. They touched her face with a Hue-bathed hand and whispered, *"Alinare."*

She heaved a heavy sigh of relief as the spell worked its magic and she fell asleep.

An ambulance quickly appeared. Romy showed the medics their magic license. After taking a brief moment to explain the situation, they tried to learn more about what could be going on. "Have you heard anything about this place? Any weird stories or strange happenings?"

"My girlfriend's a mage, actually," one of them responded while placing a still unconscious Karen on a gurney. "She told me how fucked up this place was. Said a whole mess of mages were called, but all of them ran scared."

They rubbed the bridge of their nose. "Fabulous…"

"You think you can handle this alone?"

"Of course," They lied.

✳ ☽ 4 ☾ ✳

A haunting of this level required an incredible amount of cooperative magic, but since the place was blacklisted that would be impossible. Thus, Romy was forced to think outside the box. They pulled out their phone and called the only person they knew who could help. Alfie Pugh, resident empath of the Boston Area Mental Health Co-Op and their roommate.

"You are very lucky," he told Romy over the phone in his typical near-robotic monotone. "I had a last-minute cancellation."

"Yeah, I'm suuuuper lucky," they said, sarcastically.

A long pause told Romy that Alfie was confused. "That is what I said, yes."

"I was being sarcastic, Alf."

Another long pause. "Okay."

"How soon can you get here?"

"I would need to take a ride share, so that is dependent on the availability of the drivers, the speed and skill of the driver once summoned, as well as the location of the house by way of my own. Would you be willing to pay half of my travel fees?"

Romy was losing patience. "Yes, Alfie, just get here." They turned their attention back to the EMT while pulling their business card out from their sleeve. "When she wakes up, can you call me?"

"Of course. She'll be at All Saints Hospital."

"Great. Thanks. Take care of her."

And off they drove.

While waiting for Alfie to show up, they began to investigate the house and try to figure out why the haunting was so intense. Yet nothing suspicious arose in their findings. No homicides, suicides, or any other mystical incidents. Which only deepened the mystery.

Romy remembered Karen mentioning that she thought her mother was the ghost, so they looked up her obituary: Edith Rose. Died of a heart attack, aged 92. Former nurse. Widowed shortly before her only daughter was born.

'But none of this feels like a well-meaning-old-woman-style haunting... this is some hidden burial ground, defiled-grave shit.'

After thirty minutes of waiting, Alfie eventually called back.

"Hey, where are you?" Romy said while rocking back and forth on the front porch's swing bench, resisting the urge to burst into tears from the potent negativity emanating from the house.

His usually bright Welsh accent was bogged down by what sounded like incredible stress and strain. "I am two blocks away, and unable to progress. There is an absurd amount of emotional energy in the area. I fear I may suffer an aneurysm should I get closer."

Not to be deterred, Romy thought up a quick solution. "Okay, gimme a second."

"I fear you would need to take longer than that."

"I meant give me some time."

"Okay. How much time?"

"Alfie…"

"Okay."

Romy put their phone down, activated their Hue, and started running around the house, burning psychic ward sigils on every entry point the house had. Windows, doors, even the smallest of air vents.

"How about now?" They asked Alfie over the phone.

"Better. Not perfect, yet I believe I can now progress."

A few moments later, they were face to face. Alfie's antennae were frantically twitching. He was stimming. Something that happened anytime his empathic powers were stretched to their limit.

Alfie was not a typical psychic. Alfie was not a typical person. Alfie was an extraterrestrial - a native of Planet Nine in the neighboring star system of Proxima Centauri, adopted into an Earthling family when his empathic powers made him unwanted on his home planet.

To the benefit of blending in, he looked almost like an Earthling save for a few key differences. Lime green skin, curly mint green hair, a pair of antennae poking out of his forehead with phosphorescent tips, with equally luminescent pink eyes. And his sweat smelled of rotted fruit. Most days, he passed as an imp or a nymph.

His powers, being both extraterrestrial and mutant in nature, were unique and incredulous. He could sense the emotions of anyone in a half-mile radius. As a result, he had to work mighty hard to maintain a calm and centered mind. His skill with this power, honed through training with many powerful psychics, granted him enough talent to provide intense psychic therapy at the local counseling center. He took clients of all backgrounds and pay scales but gave Romy a special dispensation for assisting with hauntings.

He was wearing his usual attire – a salmon pink button-up shirt with matching pants. He rarely strayed from this as he was very particular about his appearance. He had seven shirts and seven pants, all nearly completely identical to one another, a sign of his less than standard nature.

After a few moments of adjusting, he finally spoke. "Just so you know, between getting out of the car and now, the psychic energy radiating from within the house has gotten stronger. I believe your wards are already weakening." Romy gave a look of discomfort. "And your spike in anxiety informs me that is worse than I anticipated."

"It means the poltergeist is getting stronger."

"And thus, we must act quickly."

✳ ☽ 8 ☾ ✳

"Indeed."

"What would you have me do?"

"I need to perform an exorcism. And whatever is haunting this place is quite possibly one of the angriest, most violent spirits I've ever encountered."

"You need me to grief counsel the spirit so you can force it to move on. However," His antennae started twitching again. "There is more than one mind inside that house."

"I figured." Romy summoned several ward sigils and created a wall to protect them long enough to continue forming their plan. "Can you give me a head count?"

Alfie closed his eyes, and his antennae began to twitch even more ferociously. "Twelve."

Their soil brown eyes widened. "Heathen Gods…"

"That is unusual?"

"Very. Twelve angry ass spirits haunting a house for reasons I can't figure out. Not a great position to be in."

"And if you cannot figure it out, you cannot exorcise them."

"So…" They put on an apologetic face.

He could sense what was coming. "You need me to go inside with you."

"Yeah. I'm sorry."

"I know. I also know that this is important."

Alfie pulled out a small pill bottle. "Acetaminophen. It will assist." He swallowed well over the prescription dosage of pills. "We may now go inside."

"Awesome."

Romy opened the front door, unleashing a tornado of ghastly energy into the world. A cacophony of hatred, sadness, and pain filled their minds. So much so that Romy found it hard to maintain their Focus.

"Alfie, I need you to help."

"How may I assist?"

"I need you to make me feel very confident right now."

"Wonderful idea. I will do my best." With great mental fortitude, Alfie managed to straighten out their antennae and home in on Romy. Despite all the spells and sigils tattooed on their body to prevent such an invasion, their mind quickly opened up to him and, with brilliant swiftness, he was able to bring out all of their confidence and conviction.

Immediately feeling the effects, Romy's Hue lit up brilliantly and they were able to cast an incredible shield against the devilish energy. With this protecting them, the two forced their way into the living room.

"Now, how do you feel about a little astral projection?"

"It has been some time, but it is much like, how one would say, riding a bicycle. Which is ironic since I cannot ride a bicycle."

"Just sit down and hold my hands."

Alfie did as he was told. "What now?"

"Release your astral form and I'll follow. We need to communicate with our little dirty dozen so we can figure out what the problem is. Okay?"

But they received no response. Alfie's mind had already left his body. Romy knew they had to quickly follow.

"Release the mind. Leave form behind. Release the mind. Leave form behind. Eliberare." And out they went into...

The astral plane. A realm of pure thought directly parallel to the physical plane, which held a version of the house, albeit a more rancid and defiled copy. The pleasant, mediocre pink wallpaper had been replaced by an insidious bile green. The paintings were all burned. The furniture looked molded, and all the mirrors and picture frames were broken, leaving the shattered glass to float about like snowflakes.

Alfie greeted them. "I forgot that this is how you see yourself, Romy."

Romy looked at themself and saw that they were dressed in a ripped-up straitjacket. A reflection of some inner turmoil brought upon by the plane's abstract nature. However, unlike Romy, Alfie looked exactly as he did in the real world. A reflection of his incredibly stable sense of self.

"What shall we do next?" Alfie asked.

Romy focused with great intent and changed their astral clothing to resemble what they were physically wearing.

"The ghosts. It'll be easier to deal with them here. We find them, figure out what they want, and then get them to move on."

"Is an exorcism ever truly that easy, Romy?"

"No, removing ghosts is that easy. The exorcism involves me violently forcing the spiritual manifestation of the ghosts' lingering emotional attachment to the mortal world back to the Aether where it belongs."

Astral Alfie looked puzzled. "That sounds unpleasant."

"It will be."

"I've always wanted to ask, what is the difference between a ghost and a poltergeist?"

"Can I explain while we search?"

"I do not know, can you?"

Alfie wasn't trying to be pedantic. Alfie was just pedantic. It was a sad, yet hilarious, symptom of his social ineptitude.

"Excuse me. May I explain while we search?"

"Of course."

The two began to explore the astral version of the house.

"Ghosts are just what you probably think they are. A dead person's soul is stuck in the mortal realm to resolve unfinished business. Poltergeists happen when a ghost's intentions are less than savory and the aether - magical energy - tethering them to this world starts to produce a curse that infects whatever area they choose to haunt."

"So, if a ghost stays in this world for too long it can become a poltergeist?"

"A good metaphor would be if you let an infection become too serious and then all of a sudden your doctor has to amputate your leg."

"The slippery slope of human physical and mental health extends even beyond their mortal existence. How interesting."

"You don't have ghosts on your home planet?"

"Not that I know of. I spent very little time there before I was adopted and brought to live here."

"How old were you?"

The two came upon the kitchen and began to search there.

"Two earth years." He opened the door to the basement and a great psychic scream sent his astral form back into his body.

Romy quickly re-joined him in the mortal plane. "Are you okay?"

"My head hurts. Also, I believe we must check the basement."

With Alfie super-charging Romy's confidence-based Focus – the very emotional center of their ability to access and control their magic – and Romy super-charging their wards, the two slowly and steadily made their way through to the door to the basement. Despite all that they were doing to resist the monstrous force, it kept creeping into their minds. They began to hear voices.

"It's better this way. It's better this way. It's better this way." Like nails on a chalkboard, these screeching, piercing voices would chant throughout the hallways of their heads. *"It's better this way. It's better this way. It's better this way."*

"I believe they want us to help."

"That's usually how this goes down. Ghosts want to resolve their issues. Poltergeists convince them it's impossible, and that makes them angry and violent."

The two slowly made their way down the stairs, and the chanting became louder and more bone-chilling. *"It's better this way. It's better this way. It's better this way."*

"Once again, I must express confusion. Are ghosts and poltergeists separate beings, or not?"

"The human soul is complicated. Particularly when you factor in magic and spirits and curses."

"Are human souls different from spirits?"

"That is a completely different conversation altogether."

"This is confusing."

"You're tellin' me?"

"Yes. I am."

They finally made it to the bottom of the stairwell, finding an empty basement. There, the chanting became even louder. *"It's better this way. It's better this way. It's better this way."*

However, the voices also became more distinct. Enough so for the two to divine what they were.

"Children." Alfie said, out loud.

"Twelve children. No wonder this is such a problematic situation."

"No, only eleven children. I can distinctly hear the voices of eleven separate children."

"But there are twelve ghosts."

"Yes, but one is silent. And children make hauntings more problematic?"

"Like I said, ghosts have unfinished business. For adults, that business is more coherent. Buried treasure. A lost will. 'There's money in the banana stand.' But children are naturally unpredictable and easily confused. And it's even worse when they're dead. They may have unfinished business but they're too disoriented to figure out what it could be. And with all of these voices, all of these souls overlapping each other…"

"A poltergeist was created."

"You're catching on."

Alfie looks at them quizzically. "I have caught nothing." Romy gave them a look. "Figure of speech. Understood."

Romy thought quickly. "Do you think you can communicate with them?"

"I do not know. I can hear them, obviously, but I do not know if they have the capacity to listen to me."

"Hmm… we need to go back to the astral plane."

"That did not work so well the first time."

"Then we're going to need to set the proper tone." Romy summoned another glyph and burned it into the floor beneath them.

"What is that?"

"It's something that's going to help." They sat down on the ground again and signaled for Alfie to join them. "C'mon."

Alfie did as he was told and grabbed Romy's hands as they activated their Hue and the glyph beneath them glowed a brilliant magenta.

The two were once again in the astral plane, but this time, instead of the house, they found themselves in what appeared to be a primary school room. Fourteen chairs were placed in an even circle. There were children's toys and books scattered about, alphabet wallpaper, and a single door.

"You manipulated the manifestation of the plane to create a literal safe space inside an abstract safe space." Alfie couldn't help but admire the brilliance. "I am going to counsel them in a psychic counseling center."

"That's what you're good at. Sit down."

Alfie took a seat. "Are you going to invite them in?"

Romy walked to the door. "They want us to help. I hope they're willing to let us help them on our terms. The longer they stay here, the worse it'll be for them."

Alfie sighed. "Alright. Open the door."

Romy opened the entrance door, and eleven children quietly entered the room. All between the ages of five and seven. All wearing hospital gowns. And all children of color, either black or Latine. They looked nervous and unsure of what to do.

"Please," Alfie said. "Take a seat."

Quietly, and without any fuss, each sat down, leaving two seats open. The thirteenth for Romy, and the fourteenth for the last soul, who had yet to show themself.

"Normally, in these kinds of situations, I would have us all go around the circle and introduce ourselves. However, I can sense that some of you do not fully remember who you are. Know that there is no shame in this. You have been through much, and to come before me today shows great strength."

Recognizing that Alfie had the situation with the children under control, Romy went about finding the poltergeist, which they presumed to be the twelfth ghost.

They left the room and found themself in a decrepit hospital hallway. Insidiously flickering fluorescent lights all seemed to be leading them down towards a door marked "12." It was covered in fungus, mold, composed of rotted, soiled wood, with barbed wire covering the handle.

They grabbed the handle and could feel the fingernails of every child in the therapy room clawing at their psyche. They pushed through the psychic pain, and opened the door, rushing inside. There, they found an elderly woman, strapped to a hospital bed, struggling against her restraints, screaming through a gag made of jump rope.

Romy walked slowly over to her, unsure of whether or not she was truly an old woman's ghost or a demonic spirit in a clever disguise. They removed her gag, then cast a question spell, one that must be answered with the absolute truth.

"Cum te numeşti?"

"My name is Edith Rose." She spoke with a bloody, toothless mouth. "Please, help me."

"I will, if you answer my questions."

"Please. You must help me. I just want to go home."

"You are home, Edith. This is all an illusion created by the other ghosts - the children - who went to great lengths to make sure you felt as helpless and scared as they were. Is it working?"

"Why are you doing this to me? I didn't do anything wrong." She started to cry.

"Then why are they trapping you here? What did you do to them?"

"I didn't do anything."

Another question spell. "Ce le-ai făcut."

"I killed them!" She screamed. "I killed them!"

Romy wasn't shocked. They wanted to be, but they weren't. The minute they saw the children in hospital gowns, they knew she, Edith Rose, former nurse, was responsible for all of this.

"Why? The sooner you tell me, the sooner you can get out of this and move on. And you want to move on, don't you?"

"I can't move on!"

"Yes, you can."

"No, I can't!" Her voice became heavy and grated, and her eyes began to glow a bright white. A whiteness that soon consumed the room and overwhelmed Romy.

When their senses returned to them, she was gone. Her restraints had been ripped apart. They quickly ran back out into the hallway, to the therapy room only to find it locked.

"Alfie?!" They banged on the door. "Alfie?! Are you okay?!"

"Everything is going to be fine," a gentle, young voice said.

Romy turned and saw a beautiful but toothless young woman, honey blonde hair done up in a tight bun, wearing a nurse's uniform, dated to be from around the 1970's. Edith.

"Edith. Let me see the children."

She sighed. "Trust me. It's better this way."

The chanting resumed. The voices of the children echoed through the hallway. "It's better this way. It's better this way. It's better this way."

She smiled. "And it sounds like they agree with me."

"I think we both know that's not true. Their unfinished business was exposing you for the monster that you are. The monster that killed them. Your unfinished business is making sure that nobody ever does."

"I'm not a monster," she said in a calm, empty, nurse's voice.

"Tell that to the kids whose souls you've trapped in this nightmare."

"I was saving them."

"From what?"

"Their parents. They couldn't take care of them. One by one, these poor, unfortunate, cursed little darlings would come to the hospital with broken bones, bruises, infections. Obvious signs of neglect. Some came from broken homes. Their mothers working three jobs just to put moldy slices of bread and cheese on the table. None of them had any chance of a proper future. No quality of life. Truly, what would you have done?"

"I probably would've started with not murdering them."

Her eyes turned white, and her voice became deep and grated. "It was not murder." And then she returned to normal. "It was mercy."

Romy's brown eyes began to glow magenta as they activated their Hue. The world shifted and they were back in the house, restored to how it looked when Edith was still alive, and at the height of her killing spree.

She was in her kitchen, a strange concoction brewing over the stove.

"A potion," Romy pointedly remarked.

"Medicine."

"But you're not a witch."

"Thank the Good Lord, no. But I knew where to find one that specialized in these kinds of home remedies."

Romy took a closer look and saw what she was doing. "You made a digestible natural causes curse. Killing them while making it look like it was the result of an illness or natural defect."

"Killing them with kindness."

They looked in the corner and saw an 8-year-old Karen, looking scared and full of sadness as she watched her mother brew.

"And she was involved, how?"

The room shifted again. Back to the hospital. This time, Edith is talking to the mother of one of the kids.

"You know, I can tell you're overworked. My daughter, Karen, is just about your son's age. Why don't you let him come over and play with her while you're out working? Maybe then you can keep your boy out of trouble."

The mom looked relieved.

Another shift. A child Karen playing with one of the children in the backyard. Edith came outside to serve them lemonade, laced with the concoction.

"You put your blood in the mix, knowing it would keep Karen from getting poisoned."

"You truly are a wonder."

"But they never connected the deaths to you. How?"

"Oh, a dozen reasons. My word against theirs. An upstanding member of the community, a caregiver, an attentive mother, a widow, being accused of witchcraft by an uneducated woman who couldn't afford a babysitter. Back then, you couldn't be a mage and work in a hospital. It simply wasn't done."

"So, there were records that proved you weren't a witch. And that kind of potion doesn't leave much of a trace. So, why are you still here?"

They were back in the basement.

"I'm here because these ungrateful children have trapped me here. Please." She transformed back into an old woman. "Help me."

"No, you're here because there's something that can link you to these murders."

Edith became visibly enraged as her eyes turned a bright white. "I'm asking you nicely, young man. Help me get rid of these children."

"No, they will not." Alfie had appeared, with all eleven children standing strong behind him. "Would you like to show them what we have learned, children?"

They all watched as a memory of young Karen rushed down the stairs, holding something precious tight in her fist. She came to the center of the basement and loosened a floorboard, revealing a hiding spot home to a small box. She opened it, exposing a collection of baby teeth. Edith could be heard talking to the mother of one of the children, gushing about how wonderful her child was. With her mother distracted, Karen placed the tooth she had been holding in her hand in the box before replacing it back in its hiding spot and running upstairs.

Turning back to their murderer, each of the children opened their mouths, revealing a missing baby tooth each.

"Clever girl," Romy remarked. "The potion dissolves in their system but would stick to a tooth if it were removed quickly. And the potion has your blood in it… I wonder how she found that out."

Another scene change. Karen was reading the potion's instructions in the middle of the night.

Romy smirked and chuckled softly. "Even your daughter knew how evil you were."

Edith's white eyes became more intense as they all returned to the basement. "She didn't understand."

"So, you made her understand, I'm assuming."

The sounds of a crying Karen against the heavy beating of a belt slapped in the background. "Mommy, stop! I promise, I won't tell!"

"Nobody could understand."

"Oh, I'm sure they will. Alfie, I think it's time we-"

"NO!" Edith's voice became deep, grated, and demonic once more. Her skin shriveled and her hair thinned until she looked like a ghoul. A full-fledged Poltergeist, her appearance finally reflecting the demon she was inside.

Her clawed hands stretched across the astral room to grab Romy and Alfie by the necks.

The children, terrified, ran to hide.

"Romy," Alfie struggled. "I cannot return to my body."

"YoU wIlL nEvEr Go BaCk!" The ghoul screeched.

Romy was overwhelmed. They didn't know what to do. So, they acted on instinct, clawing at the creature's hand only for it to tighten around their neck.

Alfie looked over and tried to reach for their friend. They watched as Romy's eyes began to flicker their glowing magenta only to fizzle out. He tried reaching out with his mind but found something strange within.

The poltergeist's grip tightened around their necks even more. Romy's eyes responded by filling the room with a brilliant magenta light. Their Hue had overcome everything.

The two were back in the physical world. In the basement of the house. As was the poltergeist. Alfie looked up and saw Romy floating a foot above the ground, their body glowing brilliantly, hands outstretched towards the demon. Its legs were straightened, and arms outstretched, magically crucified.

Alfie watched as what looked like a rod made of magenta light began to appear in front of Romy. And then, Romy quietly uttered, *"Izgoni."*

The creature screamed like metal grinding on rust. Alfie felt like his ears were bound to bleed. He watched as the spirit was overwhelmed by bolts of magenta lightning erupting from the staff before being burned out of existence.

With their mission accomplished, Romy fell to the ground. Unconscious.

"Romy?" Alfie crawled over to them. He could sense they were still alive, but their mind was flying around in a thousand different directions. Not knowing what else to do, Alfie slapped them.

"OUCH!" They yelled as they came to.

"I apologize!"

"No, it's fine. I'll admit, I was a little lost there."

"You were still in the astral plane?"

"Someone had to check in on them." Romy crawled over to the infamous floorboard and pulled out the box.

The ghosts of the children manifested before them. Smiling. No longer scared. Alfie felt them all at once.

"They are so happy." A tear came to his eyes.

Romy's eyes joined Alfie's with joyful tears as they held the box. "It's okay, guys. Everything is gonna be okay."

With the ghostly sounds of joyous laughter and cheers, they faded away.

"What should we do now?" Alfie asked.

Romy drove them to the hospital where Karen was resting in the E.R. She looked pleased to see them. She could sense a change in the air.

"It's over?" she asked, weakly. "She's gone?"

"Yes," Romy confirmed. "She can't hurt you anymore. Or them."

They placed the box of teeth on her tray in front of her.

She started to cry. "Oh... my friends. I'm so sorry."

"Do not be sorry," Alfie said. "They trusted you. They knew you could do the right thing."

"But I didn't." Karen sniffled. "Even after she died... I couldn't."

Romy couldn't help but sympathize. "Recognizing that someone you love is a monster is hard. It's hard to admit to yourself. It's hard to admit to somebody else."

"Yet remember, it was you who reached out for help. It was you who truly saved them."

"No. I didn't. I killed them. For so many years... for so long, I wanted to bring them peace. I could feel them, with me, wherever I went. They came to me in my dreams. They begged me. But I couldn't. She was too strong. And I... I was a coward."

Alfie touched her hand. "You are not a coward. Because of you, they are at peace now. And they want you to be too."

"You can take these to the police. Everyone will finally know what really happened. Their families can be at peace now too."

Her tears of pain turned to tears of joy. She hugged the treasure box close to her chest.

"Thank you. Thank you both, so much."

"You are more than welcome." Romy smiled and gestured to Alfie that it was time to go.

As they walked back to Romy's car, Alfie held a curious but familiar question in his mind. "Romy, you know you did it again, right?"

"Did what?"

"Summoned the staff?"

"What staff?"

"You summoned a staff earlier when you banished the poltergeist."

"What? No, I didn't. I used a very simple casting. A little old lady isn't exactly a ferocious monster."

"That was not a simple casting. And I dare say that 'little old lady' was quite the definition of a ferocious monster. I may not have much knowledge when it comes to spells, but it did look quite complicated."

"I mean, it may have just looked like that to you, but it was no big deal."

Alfie started to sense a strange phenomenon surrounding Romy's mind. With a quiet, benign probe, he found that they had no memory of casting that spell. Their mind's eye was in the process of fabricating an entirely different version of events. One that completely contradicted all that he had witnessed, perfectly preserved by his photographic memory. A mental phenomenon that occurred within Romy whenever anything like this happened. A mental phenomenon that fascinated the cerebral Alfie to no end.

They were gaslighting themself.

"Well, I guess there is no point in belaboring this subject. I do say, do you not have an appointment to keep?"

Romy looked at the time on their phone. "Ugh. Fuck. I was hoping this whole thing would've cut straight through that ridiculousness."

"It is just a date, Romy. I am sure it will be lovely. Guy is actually very excited to meet you."

"Guy? His name is Guy? Neither of you told me his name was Guy. What kind of a name is that?"

"Romy, you are truly an enigma."

2

Moving On

'He was s'posed to be here at five… clearly, I have been stood up,' Romy thought to themself as they sat, alone, in Ruthy's Diner. Out of nerves, they had arrived an hour early and drank through so many free soda refills the server was now charging them.

The stress they had endured all day, leading up to this moment, had made them a mess. After the exorcism ordeal, they went home and changed between a dozen different outfits before deciding on their standard casual look. A black tee that exposed their skinny, tattooed arms; shredded, faded black skinny jeans; combat boots. For added originality, they painted their nails a glossy pink on every finger save for their pinkies, which remained black. Topping off the look were their favorite accessories – a crow's foot pendant made from their childhood familiar, Blinken, and a pair of magician's handcuffs they had turned into bracelets.

They thought back on the circumstances of how they came to be on this date. Besides the bus. The truth: it was their *stupid roommates*. Alfie and Kass. They had both become obnoxiously obnoxious since Romy had "mutually separated" from their partner of almost a decade.

"Mutually separated?" Kass would counter, mockingly, her voice an astounding combination of honey sweet and nail clipper sharp. "Baby, you got dumped."

It was hers and Alfie's idea for Romy to come on this blind date.

"Alfie says he has a work buddy who is very interested," Kass told them while they were studying the latest issue of Necromancer Monthly.

"By the Heathen Gods, excuse me if I don't trust *Alfie's* taste in men."

She stood her ground in their bedroom doorway. "He says he's really sweet and really cute."

"I'm not interested in dating anybody," Romy said as they tried to read.

"Who says date? I say fuck. Fuck until you can't see straight. Or, in your case, can't see gay. Fuck until *what's-his-face* falls out of your memory forever. Capisce?"

"Me and 'what's-his-face' were together for a third of our lives. You don't just fuck anyone after that."

"Alfie says that you're suffering from self-protective psychosomatic behavior borne from your intense abandonment issues."

They dropped their magazine and pointed their nose at Kass. "Alfie needs to mind his own fucking business."

"I think we both know Alfie can't do that."

Romy could not help but become enticed. "How cute are we talking?"

Kass showed them a picture on her phone. "This cute."

The man in the picture was model gorgeous. Almond skin, shirtless, muscular, dark blond hair that Romy suspected was a dye-job, smiling like a doctor just told him he would live forever, and posed with a guitar in his strong arms.

"That can't be real. It has to be an ad for sunblock or something."

"Romy, Alfie took this picture."

"Why is he shirtless?"

"Apparently he likes being shirtless."

"Again, that can't be real."

"Baby, this is a *real* person, and he is *really* interested in meeting you."

"That cannot possibly be true."

"Why not?"

"He is way too hot for me."

Kass gave them a heavy stare. "Bitch, you are hot too. Calm down and get on this."

So, there they were, waiting for one of their roommate's work colleagues with the intention – the incredible hope – that he would be the rebound that gets them through the next few lonely years.

The sound of a bell ringing. Romy looked up and there he was. Shoulder-length dark blond hair pulled into a ponytail. Sky blue eyes shining through wire-framed glasses. Deeply sun-kissed arms peeking out of a B-52's novelty shirt with the sleeves cut off. Somehow, he had managed to look better in person than in his picture. Something as rare as a unicorn.

"Well, fuck…" Romy accidentally said aloud.

The absurdly gorgeous man's absurdly gorgeous blue eyes scanned the room, met Romy's, and smiled that sunshine smile from the photo. Romy swooned and forgot their ex's name for a few seconds. Carrying a guitar case, he awkwardly walked through the narrow passages between tables and booths to get to them.

"Sorry, I'm late," he said, still smiling like sunshine, his voice like butter on a warm biscuit. Delicious in every way possible. "Work ran over and then car troubles and ugh… I'm sorry."

Romy stood up like they were meeting a prince. And for all they knew, he could have been one. 'Kiss me, and wake me up, you gorgeous man…'

"I'm Guy," the gorgeous man said as he pulled Romy into a tight, warm hug.

'Oh, Heathen Gods, he's like a human sunbeam.'

"I'm Romy." Romy started fiddling with their crow's foot, with a flirtatious sort of air. "You work at the counseling center with Alfie, right?"

Guy took a moment to look Romy up and down. He didn't say anything, but his face said, "You are gorgeous."

Romy began to feel naked. "Guy?"

He snapped out of it. "What? Oh. Yeah, I do music therapy."

"Maybe we should sit down." Romy said with a coy smile.

"Yeah, smart idea." The two sat down across from each other. "Alfie didn't tell me what you do though."

Feeling a sudden urge to show off, Romy decided to have a little fun. "I'll give you one guess." With a flick of their wrist, and a gleam of magenta-colored magic in their eyes, the water jug lifted itself off the table and gracefully filled Guy's empty glass.

The trick worked as his face gave away his bedazzlement. "Wow! You're in the magic trade?"

"Yup, got my degree and everything."

"That's so cool. B-T-W, what is the proper gender-neutral term for a magical person?"

"Well, it's normally mage but I prefer necromancer since it's what I do."

"You necromance? How *necromantic*."

"Wow, you are *so clever*," they said with playful sarcasm in their voice.

"Got my degree and everything," he said with a twinkle in his eye. "I don't know very many mages. Where do you go to school for something like that?"

"Harvard," they said nonchalantly.

Guy was stunned and impressed. "You went to Harvard?!"

"What, like it's hard?"

"What about high school and stuff?"

"Well, it's a general custom to get trained by your coven before choosing a magical college. And there's only, like, three of those in the country."

He leaned in, fascinated. "Coven?"

"Another word for magical family."

"Does your magical family include any siblings?"

"Two," they said, trying to hide the dark feelings that arrived anytime they discussed their family.

"That's a healthy amount."

"You?"

"Only child. I wish I had siblings though. Would've made my childhood less boring."

Romy's voice lowered. "There are downsides, trust me. Especially in a magical family…"

"Oh, do tell."

'Well, here it goes.' Romy opened their familial can of worms with a sigh, reminding themself not to overshare. "Well, for instance, my big sister 'accidentally' set me on fire on my tenth birthday… and one time, my little brother teleported our shared bedroom into the backyard."

"Wow… that does… sound like a lot."

The server arrived and dropped their menus on the table. "Good evening, everybody. I'm Alicia, I'll be your server. Just so you know, we have a special on pie tonight so it's two slices for the price of one."

"Thanks," Guy said, continuing to brighten the room with his sunshine smile.

Knowing that Romy had already had enough to drink, their focus turned to Guy. "And can I get *you* anything to drink before you're ready to order?"

"I'm good with water for now, thanks. Do you want anything to drink, Romy?"

Their voice lowered even further out of shame. "Trust me, I'm good."

"Okey-dokey, I'll check back in with you boys in a few minutes."

Romy cringed. They hated being misgendered. Worse yet, they hated how maybe they were too "masc presenting" to signal that their identity did not align with their birth-assigned sex. 'Am I not dressing queer enough?' they would ask themselves whenever someone called them "bro", or "sir", or, worse yet, "daddy." At the end of it all, though, they knew it was a simple lack of knowledge about the existence of genders that exist outside the male-female binary. As far as Romy knew, only a fraction of a fraction of a fraction of the world's population were people who identified as non-binary. Thus, they simultaneously expected people to assume their gender while still recoiling every time they do.

Guy stopped the server. "Actually, they're non-binary. Their pronouns are they-them, so they're not a boy."

"Oh, gosh, I'm so sorry," they said with a flustered face. "I'm so-so-so-so sorry. I didn't mean to- I am so sorry."

"It's okay," Romy said, more focused on how sexy Guy's foray into allyship was than the overly apologetic server.

As they retreated to the kitchen, Guy turned back to Romy. "So, necromancy, that's dead people magic, right?"

"Yeah," they said with an impressed smile.

"What all do you do?"

"It depends on the day. It could be something as simple as getting a dead relative on the line so someone can find out where a priceless antique is, or it could be something as extreme as an exorcism."

His face turned from sun to moon in a microsecond. "Woof, poltergeists, yeesh."

"You're familiar?"

"Bad childhood experience. We actually ended up moving. Even after the exorcism, the house still felt just way too creepy to live in."

"Yeah, geists can be the worst."

"How do 'geists' even happen?"

"I feel like telling you wouldn't make the fact that you lived with one for a while any better on your memory."

He nodded. "I'll take your word on it."

"I've created a couple zombies in my day. One time, I had to fuse a guy's soul to a painting. That was entertaining as hell."

"Why?"

"Why what?"

"Zombies… painting… why?"

"My method of making money is very strange. It's best not to focus on it."

Guy blinked hard. "Valid."

They smiled. "Let's focus on eating and getting to know each other and staring longingly into each other's eyes."

"'Longingly?'" He laughed a princely laugh. "You are adorable."

Dinner went by smoothly. Burgers. Fries. Pie that Server Alicia offered entirely on the house as a part of her continued apology. And then it turned into a dreamy stroll along the pier.

"Favorite food?" Guy asked.

"Stroganoff."

He beamed. "Beef and noodles? Yum."

"How 'bout you?"

"I'm a sucker for my dad's borscht."

"Borscht?!" Romy shuddered just thinking about such a delicacy.

He was only half-seriously taken aback. "I'm sorry. Is there something wrong with borscht?"

"It's beet soup. Is there something right with it?"

"Listen, bub, if you're wanting a second date, you're gonna have to stop trash talking my favorite food."

Romy put up their hands in false surrender. "Oh no, please forgive me."

They laughed together before sitting on a nearby bench. Guy's gaze met Romy's and his piercing blue eyes threatened to burn a hole through their skull.

"So," Romy continued, "what are your parents like?"

Guy's face fell, though he still held his smile. "They're actually… not with us anymore."

"Oh, by the Heathen Gods, I'm so sorry."

"It's okay. It's not like I can't talk about them. They were great. Attentive, kind, encouraging, overprotective as hell."

"How long has it been?"

"Almost ten years. After the whole geist situation, my family sold our house and moved way out to the middle of nowhere Colorado. And then… well…"

Romy could tell he didn't want to talk about what happened. "What were they like?"

He brightened up. "They were the best. My dad and his cooking. My mom and her plain, utter ridiculousness. It's the weirdest things that you miss, you know? Like how my mom would yell at me in Spanish, then yell at me louder when I yell back in English." He chuckled, lightly.

"Your mom spoke Spanish?"

"First generation Mexican immigrant. One of the best immigration attorneys at large. And my dad was the best chef, still can't find anybody – pro or otherwise – that can match his recipes. I like to pretend I'm good at cooking too but really all I do is read my dad's old cookbook like the dictionary."

"Your parents sounded like a dream. Mine were... not a dream."

"I'm sorry. Is all this family talk triggering something I should be cautious about?"

"It's okay. I'm mostly over the messy childhood."

"Same." And then, he bravely asked, "What's your opinion of kissing on the first date?"

Romy responded by putting their arm around his shoulders and pulling him into what would seem like a kiss to the outside world but could only be described as a moment of pure magic. The heat of their lips together ignited a spark within both of them. A spark that quickly turned into an inferno that swept them up and somehow transported them back to Guy's studio apartment.

Clothes were quickly discarded as Guy led the two of them to his bed.

Between kisses, he managed to eke out, "When were you last tested?"

"Two weeks ago." Romy felt the need to get tested after Nico left, paranoid that perhaps he'd cheated on them. "Negative. You?"

"Two months. Negative. On PreP."

"You got condoms?"

"Bottom drawer, next to the bed."

"Top or bottom?"

"Vers-bottom. Which basically just means bottom," he giggled.

"How convenient. I'm a top."

"I love tatted up tops."

"I love twunk bottoms."

"How do you feel about blowjobs?"

"Love'em."

Soon after this, Romy was flat on their back on the bed with Guy graciously going down on them. They were so overcome that they could only keep one word in their mind. 'Inferno. Inferno. Inferno.' This mental exercise was a wonderful method at keeping them from climaxing too soon. Guy's efforts and abilities were impressive.

He resurfaced. "You're pre-cumming quite a bit, you know. Am I going too fast?"

"Trust me," Romy said between heavy breaths. "You're perfect."

All of a sudden, his face became contorted as an awkward thought crossed his mind. "Hey, will you excuse me for a moment?"

"Sure."

And in a flash, they saw Guy's perky rear escape into the bathroom. Perplexed, they had to put some thought into what was so urgent. Then it came to them. 'Oh yeah… he was at work before we met up… poor thing. He has to douche.'

Given the time, Romy found themselves taking in the apartment. A television with every gaming console that existed in the world attached to it. An electronic drum set, a bass guitar, and an electric guitar all assembled in the odd corner. An immense number of posters of various bands and video game characters were strewn about the room like wallpaper. It all ended with a bedside table with a humble lamp on top of it, and a drawer that Romy knew was full of lube and sex toys.

Their phone lit up. A text from Kass: You dirty bitch ;-D Have fun!!!!

They were about to text back a smart-ass remark when a naked Guy returned from the bathroom. "Thanks for waiting."

He eagerly bounced back into bed.

"Don't worry, you're worth it," Romy said as they ran their hands through his hair and pulled him into another burning kiss. They began exploring his taut, muscular body. Running along the curves of his tender form. They kissed down his neck, chest, and stomach. They smoothly maneuvered themself down to the foot of the bed and pushed his legs up into his chest.

What was then executed with keen precision was an activity that both Romy and Guy thought was underrated: rimming. They always struggled to not use magic to please their partners. Relying on magic to do anything - least of all sexual pleasure - was a common crutch for many mages. And Romy was intent on pleasing this man without assistance.

To that end, their hand reached up to his hard cock and began to stroke it tenderly in concert with the vibrations of their tongue in his tight hole.

Overwhelmed, Guy pulled Romy up and began kissing them madly. They were pleased but shocked. Their sexual partners usually asked them to wash their mouth out after delivering a rimjob before allowing the sex to continue.

Guy roughly whispered into Romy's ear, "I want you to fuck me."

Romy wordlessly obliged, once again pushing Guy's legs into his chest before positioning themself. Guy quickly grabbed a small bottle of hemp-based "sex oil" from the bedside table.

"Are you allergic to hemp?" He asked.

"No, I'm good."

A condom was slid on while sex oil was liberally applied to both parties.

"I'm ready when you are," Guy said with an excited smile.

It had been three months, a week, and three days since Romy had last had sex with another person, and it was worth the wait. As they entered, a great sense of euphoria came over them. The inferno returned, and it threatened to melt them both.

They started off slow. Calmly pushing in and pulling out. Inch by inch. Until, finally, they had reached the point of no return. Guy had relaxed around them.

His body seized. "That's it, that's it right there, just hold it."

"Okay - okay." Romy stopped all movement.

A moment's pause. "Alright, slowly."

"Okay." Romy began to pulse slowly, which was greeted with Guy's pleasure-tinged moans. "You like that?"

"Oh yeah..." Heavy breaths. "Oh God..."

Having a little fun, Romy quickly shoved their member in as far as it could go and saw Guy's eyes nearly bug out of his head.

"Oh, God! Wow!"

"You okay?"

His face melted into a fiery smile. "I'm good. I'm good, just keep going."

He pulled them into another kiss as they picked up the pace and began pounding into him. The heat was rising. The tension was palpable. Sweat began to softly form on both bodies. Guy was gripping onto Romy for dear life, grabbing their backside and forcing it down. A clever cue to go harder, faster, and deeper.

"I'm gonna cum," He warned with a heavy voice.

"Yeah, want me to cum too?"

"Are you close?"

"Fuck yeah."

"Cum for me."

"Yeah? You want me to cum for you?"

"Yes. Please. Cum for me."

"Yeah?"

"Yeah - yeah. Oh God!" He gasped, unable to control his body as he erupted all over his stomach just as Romy made one final push and released. "Holy smokes… you are *magic*."

Romy turned to the side and fell onto the bed next to him. "Trust me. No magic was required for that." Their hands glowed a bright magenta Hue as they pulled the condom off, tossed it into the nearby trash can, and magically pulled the nearby towel towards them. "But magic is perfect for being lazy."

"Magic or not, that was very hot."

"Thank you," Romy said, awkwardly as they tried to find the right words to say. "You were… I mean… I can't even-"

He stopped them. "It's okay. I know I'm good." He laid down and put his arm around Romy, pulling them into a soft cuddle. "Hey, did you ever notice that you glow?"

"Yeah, it's my Hue."

He began stroking their arms, admiring the tattoos. "Hue? What's that?"

"It's an expression of our magic. We use our emotions to conjure the magic and release it through our Hues. Sort of like how your brain forms the words and your mouth makes them."

"That's hot."

"Is it?"

He chuckled. "Yeah! Very! So, what inspired the body art?"

"Well, believe it or not, some of these have an actual function."

"Function? Like magical function?" He asked excitedly.

"Yeah!" Romy was all too excited to show Guy the collection they had built up over the years. They began to twist and turn to show it all off. "The phases of the moon I got going on across my chest? Well, the positioning of the moon can affect magic, so this is to help regulate my power on the more problematic nights."

"What kinds of problematic nights?"

"For some reason, my powers specifically don't work that great during half-moons. So, I got the moon tats when I was fifteen."

"Fifteen?! You got that massive tattoo on your chest at fifteen?!"

"Yup!"

"And your parents were just cool with it?"

"They both have the same tattoos. You'd be hard pressed to find a mage without the standard protection sigils tattooed somewhere anybody could see them. Like this one." They gestured to the large eye on the nape of their neck. "It's the evil eye. Heightens intuition and awareness. And then there's the ouroboros." They gestured to the tattoo of the dragon eating itself wrapped around their left wrist, beneath the cuff bracelet. "Basic recycling sigil."

"Recycling?"

"Reduce and reuse all magic output."

"Is there a limit to how much magic you can use?"

"That's a longer story and I'd rather just talk about my tats."

"Okay, okay, tat on."

"There's the triquetra I got here." They pointed to the tattoo emblazoned on their left shoulder. "Reverence to the magical triad - the maiden, the mother, and the crone. And then the four symbols I have going up my forearm: wards." From wrist to shoulder. "Anti-intrusion ward, to keep people from invading my mind. Anti-possession ward, to keep ghosts from possessing me. Anti-hex ward, to keep other mages from trying to kill me. And the pro-purpose ward, in case of the need for violence, may my aim ever be true and my intentions ever clear."

Guy's eyes widened. "Need for violence? You get in fights a lot in your line of work?"

"Not as much since I moved to Boston but where I was growing up... yes..."

"Where did you grow up?"

Their voice lowered as their mind turned back to their problematic childhood. "The backwoods of Georgia."

"That sounds pleasant," he said sarcastically.

"Yeah... I get a real kick out of how aggressive and violent people think Bostonians can be. Y'all don't know 'aggressive' till you meet the bitches I grew up with... Namely, my sister."

"I'm from Southern California, so I'm used to the more passive-aggressive types. T-B-H, it's nice to meet people who say exactly what they're thinking when they're thinking it. It makes my life a lot easier."

"What part of California?"

"Hollywood."

"For real?"

"No joke. I went to school at UCLA."

"Wow," they said, trying to sound impressed.

"Yeah. And I do not miss it at all, so let's move on to talking about this tattoo." He pointed out the upward pointing pink triangle just below Romy's left breast. "Does a pink triangle have a magical meaning I'm not aware of?"

"Oh… I got this when I was seventeen and feeling dangerous."

He pulled his hand back. "How dangerous?"

Romy let out a small cackle. "It doesn't do anything."

"Then why is it dangerous?"

"Getting non-magical tattoos is a real taboo in the Coven so, rebel that I was, I got a tattoo that means nothing for no reason other than to feel special and piss my parents off. And, bitch, did it work. I didn't even know a pink triangle meant gay until I went off to college."

He laughed. "You're a rebel of the highest degree."

"And a sexy one too."

"Oh, yes, very sexy."

The two kissed. And kissed. And kissed some more. And then the kissing turned into small talk. Then the small talk turned into smaller talk as it became clear that Romy was not going home that night. And, after a few episodes of a random British comedy they both enjoyed, much to their mutual delight, the two fell asleep in each other's arms.

The next morning, Romy managed to wake up before their over-obliging host. With the grace of a crane in flight, they untangled themself from Guy's many limbs, grabbed their clothes and phone and snuck into the bathroom.

"Shit," they quietly swore as they realized that their phone had died in the night. They looked in the mirror and were impressed to find a happy looking version of themself staring back at them. They got dressed, swashed a small amount of mouthwash to get the taste of the night out of their mouth, and then cursed the Heathen Gods at their inability to make their curly, ever-rambunctious hair look less like they had just gotten laid. "Welp… fuck it. Stride of pride."

They snuck out of the bathroom, gave Guy a tender kiss on the forehead, made a mental note to text him when their phone was charged, all before gracefully making their exit. They found themself thanking the Heathen Gods that his door had an auto-lock feature.

They grabbed the train that took them to the bus that took them to the bus that took them home, where they realized they could have just called a cab.

They opened the door and was greeted with the vision of Kass, in all her morning glory, in a stunning beige silk, gold trimmed kaftan, working at her laptop on the dining room table. Her great, curly, golden-brown mane was done up in a series of ornate braids. Her great, pointed, cat ears twitched as she heard Romy walk in. Her bright yellow eyes tightened in on them as they crossed the threshold. Her big, cat-like nose gave a hefty sniff. She smiled a proud, dirty, fangy grin. "Well, good morning, you *naughty* bitch."

"Kass, at least let me shower before you slut-shame me."

"Oh, baby, I do not slut-shame. I slut-gratulate. I slut-ppreciate. I slut-lute!" She laughed at herself. "See what I did there? Like sa-lute but slut-lute."

"You're a comic genius," they said with exhausted sarcasm. "Makes me wonder why you're in security."

"Because the male dominated world of comedy could never appreciate a woman - much less a woman Sphinx - such as I to succeed in their realm of misogyny and racism. Thus, I am cursed to act as the first line of defense against the dark forces of this world."

Kassandra Al-Amin. She/Her. The most fabulous person in Romy's life.

Her long, smooth tail grabbed at her nail file on the table behind her. Handing it to herself, she began shaving at one of the many claws growing out of her fingers. Claws strong enough to cut through solid steel on a bad day.

Kass was reveling. "I mean all I can do right now is just point out how... amazing I am. I am truly wonderful. Absolutely fabulous. A genius matchmaker. Truly."

"Genius matchmaker?"

"I got you together with Guy. And that obviously worked wonders for you so, you're welcome."

"No, Alfie hooked me up with Guy."

"That may be so, but I pressured you into going out with him. So, at the end of the day, I'm responsible for your current happiness. And again, I say: you're welcome."

They wanted to argue with her, but they knew she was right. So, instead, they sighed, sniffed under their armpit, and recoiled. "I'd love to keep this conversation going but I need a shower, I need a teeth-cleaning, and I need a lot of protein."

"Yes, you do," she said, her dirty smile returning, exposing her fangs. "If you want, I can put some turkey sausage on."

"Pleeeaaase," they moaned in hunger as they slumped towards the bathroom.

Before they could even turn the sink on, a slight rumble was felt throughout the apartment.

"Romy, did you fart?" Kass joked.

"No, it must've been your mother."

The slight rumble was followed by a heavy quake as both were forced down onto the floor. To an ordinary person, this was a simple earthquake, but Romy, their soul's eyes, ears, and nose keen to the sensation of magical energy, could sense something sinister belying the sudden shift in tectonics.

It took a whole two minutes for the earthly tidal wave to subside. Romy ran over to Kass and helped her up.

"Are you okay?"

"Yeah… a little annoyed… usually I'm pretty good at seeing these things coming." The Sphinx shared many qualities with felines, including highly sensitive sensory perceptions. For instance, Kass could detect shifts in temperature that signaled rain or thunder, and the slightest movements in the earth that signaled an incoming tremor. "What the fuck was that?"

"Something not good…"

Their conversation was broken by the sounds of screams coming from outside. The two ran to the bay window in their living room and were terrified to see a sea of red clouds smothering the Boston sky. This preceded a series of great, red lightning bolts that pierced the city below, causing more quakes and tremors.

"Not good indeed," Kass said.

"Fuck…"

"Do you know what it is?"

"Necromancy. Someone's trying to summon something very big."

"Well, fuck…"

3

F-M-L

"'A state of emergency has been called-'"

The press release on television was interrupted by the door opening. Alfie entered the apartment looking worse for wear.

"You okay, sweetie?" Romy asked from their spot at the window.

He walked and talked as if he were a robot fighting off a computer virus. "Too many... emotions... work left... home... not... doing good. Help."

Romy quickly ran to the door and cast a psychic ward. *"Apel la rezistența mentală. Vatră și casă."*

A surge of magenta energy flew throughout the apartment as Romy's spell worked its magic. A relieved sigh emerged from Alfie as he flopped onto the living room couch.

"Thank you. Do they know what has happened yet?"

"It's a summoning spell."

"How do they know?"

"*I* know. It's huge - probably the work of a coven."

"Heavy concern, fear, familial-related trauma. You are repressing. Please share."

A large downside to living with Alfie was that, while the wards kept him from sensing the emotions of people outside, he could not help but accidentally keen in on Romy or Kass's mental issues.

"Alfie, I don't want to."

"Yes, you do. Also, there is a sliver of guilt and arousal in the back of your mind. Text Guy and let him know you are alright."

Romy was about to say something before realizing that they did indeed need and want to text Guy. However, before they could reach their phone, they realized something.

Alfie, sensing Romy's distress as it dawned on them, made a preemptive strike. "It is 617-555-0223."

"Thank you," They responded as they started dialing but, as they did, Kass's number buzzed at them. They answered. "What's up?"

"Just an F-Y-I, you - and probably Alfie too - are gonna get called in for a magical Conclave."

"I expected as much." They looked outside as the red sky became heavier and darker. "What's the word?"

"There is no word. My bosses' bosses are scrambling to get eyes and bodies on every VIP in the city. Meanwhile, I have been sitting outside Senator Abner's office, listening to her cry to every member of her family over the phone. And when I say I need a drink…"

She was interrupted by the beep of a second call from an unlisted number. "Shit, I think this is it. Good luck, sweetie."

"Bahibbok."

"Love you too."

She blew a raspberry into the receiver before hanging up. She was not one for getting emotional, which is why she exclusively spoke Arabic when she needed to show verbal affection. That way only the people she really cared about knew how much she cared about them.

Romy answered the other line. "Hello."

The feminine voice of a call-bot responded. "Hello. This call is to inform you that as a registered mage in the Commonwealth of Massachusetts your presence is mandated by the order of Governor Allison Reynolds as part of an ongoing investigation into a city-wide magical threat. Please arrive at Massachusetts State House with your non-expired, government issued, photo identification as well as your license to practice magic. Thank you for your cooperation and have a lovely day."

The bot hung up.

Romy knew all too well that not only was their presence "mandated" to help investigate the cataclysm, but it was also to help rat out whoever was responsible. And despite being aware of their own innocence, they were also aware that non-mages were at their worst when a magical threat arose. Suspicion and fear of the unknown brings out the worst in everyone, but when they have a small group of people to point fingers at then it only takes a single straw for all hell to break loose.

"I have a migraine," Alfie said on a loop during the hour and a half long drive to the state house. A drive which normally took less than fifteen minutes.

Meanwhile, Romy's fingers were getting tired from declining calls from the emergency bot demanding their presence at the conclave. "It's gonna be okay, Alfie. Just keep breathing and take your meds."

Traffic was bumper to bumper as police and MIST - Mystical Investigations and Security Taskforce - attempted to help with phase one evacuation efforts.

Evacuation plans in most American cities during "magical cataclysms" tended to follow the same general rubric:

1. Elderly, families with children ages 15 and below, people living with disabilities, and those without proper health or home insurance are allowed firsthand evacuation, excluding families that include licensed mages.

2. Any civilian between the ages of sixteen and 39
3. Any civilian above the age of 40 but below the age of 60
4. State officials
5. City officials
6. Emergency response workers and licensed medical professionals
7. Police
8. MIST, upon diagnosis that the magical cataclysm cannot be resolved through prescribed means
9. Licensed Mages, should any survive and upon diagnosis that the magical cataclysm cannot be resolved through magical means

The reality that they would be last out in this kind of emergency made Romy incredibly nervous. This would be their third cataclysm, which had a very loose definition in the eyes of Boston city officials.

"Any kind of magic-based citywide disturbance that may pose a potential threat, regardless of significance, to the welfare of the community."

Their first was a year after they had moved to Boston, fourteen months out of college, and ten months after they had received their license to practice magic. It was June and the weather had changed from sunny to snowy in an instant, with temperatures going below freezing as a blizzard overtook the city. The source of the unnatural disaster turned out to be a sixteen-year-old mage, adopted into a non-mage family. It was decided that, for her safety and the safety of the community, she would be handed over to a coven in California that specialized in weather regulation. It was resolved within five hours.

The second was three years after, during the fall. A large monster made out of cotton candy was wreaking havoc along the pier. MIST took it out by tossing it into the channel. The culprit had turned out to be a Troll, who attempted to use the chaos as a smokescreen to commit a series of burglaries. He is currently serving a twenty-year sentence.

Each time, Romy was called to the state house and each time, Romy didn't have to do anything. It was always resolved within a few hours. But this time, everything was different. They could feel it in the air.

"Text him," Alfie said while downing well over the prescription dose of aspirin. "The twinkle of guilt in the back of your head is like a needle in my eyeball."

Romy grunted, annoyed that their roommate knew them better than they knew themself. "Every kind of anti-invasion ward straight up tattooed on my body, and I got you giving me emotional push notifications…"

As the streets had turned into a parking lot, they felt safe pulling out their phone: Hey, sorry I haven't called or texted since I left this morning. I just wanted to let you know that I'm okay and so's Alfie. I hope evacuation goes okay for you. Please be safe. 🖤

They felt a flutter in their heart. And so did Alfie.

"You are adorable," he said.

"You are annoying," they said as a police officer motioned for them to drive into the MIST/Mage-exclusive expressway to the state house.

A few moments later they were parked in the private garage and met with a security escort. A very frantic and frenzied Kass, now appearing in her MIST uniform. A white outfit consisting of a long-sleeved top and pants with black piping lining its entirety, both made from a material specially enchanted to be resistant to both gunfire and hexes. Her name was stitched on the right breast and a great black sun was emblazoned across the back. Normally it's paired with aggressive black combat boots, but since her feet had padded bottoms and claws she was allowed to go against regulation and keep hers exposed.

"It's a fucking madhouse in there. Every mage in the tri-county area is here."

"They called in that many mages?" They asked as she led them through the maze of the state house's private entrance ways.

"Half of them just showed up on their own, actually. They felt the Aether shift and flew in on their broomsticks."

"Mages can fly broomsticks?" Alfie asked. "Romy, why did you not fly us in on a broomstick? Surely, we would have made better time…"

"Alfie, I don't have the time or the energy to go into that."

"Severe confusion, frustration, and once again an incredible amount of familial-related guilt. Kass is feeling much the same, perhaps you two should share your feelings before we initiate this level of stressful activity."

"Alfie…" the two said in accidental unison as Romy rolled their eyes.

"Anger focused on myself. I will be quiet."

They turned back to their best friend. "But, for real, are you doing okay, Kass?"

"I think we both know how much fun a room full of mages can be. Half of them keep giving me drink orders and the other half don't acknowledge me at all. Pompous dickwads."

Romy wished they could argue with Kass's assessment but, indeed, it was true. Mages, particularly Coven Mages, had developed severe superiority complexes. Particularly regarding people like Kass. Anthropomorphs, or Bestials, as they are called.

They made it to the conference room, which was baking with mystical energy. So much so that Romy thought they were going to get a fever. Neither Kass nor Alfie could feel it, but to them it was almost intoxicating. They hadn't been around that many mages since their college days.

"Well-well-well," a familiar, and incredibly unwelcome, heavy, deep, smoker's voice with hints of a Romanian accent said. "It has been too long, baby brother."

Romy was stunned to see their sister, Daciana of the Ardelean Coven. The triple threat of the magical world: necromancer, battle mage, and scholar of the highest degree. She was next in line to become the high mage of one of the most famous Necromancer covens in North America, after their father. In addition to being an expert Necromancer, she was also a notorious battlemage, famed for battling, and destroying, an entire gang of vampires. And her studies in necrotic botany as a means of reversing cell deterioration elevated and magnified a subject long thought dead. She was a living legend among the mage community and used that status to as much of an advantage as could be achieved. She was the ultimate bitch.

She wore the years well. Outside of the heavy bags under her eyes, she still retained a youthful beauty. Her mahogany brown eyes would give an ignorant mind the impression that she was gentle and wise. Her thick, dark eyebrows were unintentionally chic, as she refused to give notice to the popular culture of ordinary humans. She wore a floor length, flowing, airy black dress that blended seamlessly with her long, ebony hair which flew freely down her back.

She looked Romy up and down. "You've gained weight."

Despite their shock, they knew how to manage a confrontation with their sister. "Rather a fat ass than a fat head, I suppose."

"Well, it's my fat head that's gotten me to where I am today."

"Yes, congratulations on being mage-famous and *still* mooching off our parents."

"Oh, is that why you moved to this…" She gestured, disgustedly, with her whole body. "This…?"

"No, I moved to this," they gestured, mockingly, at everything. "Cuz of this," they gestured at Daciana.

Daciana's sharp eyes darted to Kass and Alfie. "What are these?"

"People with thoughts and feelings that you shouldn't be insulting, because they will be assisting us with this investigation. In fact, Kass is a part of MIST, who will be on the front lines if anything were to happen."

"Whatever," she said dismissively.

Then Romy had a thought. "What are you even doing here?"

"I don't have to answer that. All you need to know is that this matter will be resolved quickly now that a *qualified* mage is here." She turned her back on the conversation and, with her nose stuck firmly in the air, walked over to a group of mages huddled together in the corner.

"Alfie, are you okay?" Kass asked the empath.

Romy looked and saw that their roommate's antennae were twitching far worse than they had ever seen before. "Maybe you should go home?"

Alfie was not paying attention. He just kept twitching. "I think I should go home. I do not believe I could be of any assistance in my current state."

Unlike Kass and Romy, who met at their first cataclysm, this was Alfie's first. He had met Romy a year ago, during yet another less-than-standard haunting where he was needed to assist in counseling a less-than-standard ghost. They maintained a close friendship long enough for Alfie to fill the rental void left behind by Romy's ex-boyfriend, and the room that used to be his office.

"It's okay," Romy said, doing their best to maintain a calm facade. "I'll call if we need you."

They looked to Kass, who shook her head. "I can't leave. The amount of people I'd need to ask permission from would mean Alfie's head might explode before he got home."

Alfie looked ready to vomit. Romy had a thought. "Who's in charge?"

Kass pointed to a Centaur with long black hair, piercing silver eyes, dark skin, even darker fur, and a nose pointed to the sky. Standing at nine-and-a-half feet tall and wearing the same uniform as Kass but specially made to conform to her unique body type. Adorned with extra pips on the collar to show her seniority, she was the physical definition of commanding.

"That's Commander Lustre. And she has been doing nothing but listening to mages spout their superiority all day. So... you know... tread lightly?"

"I'll be a feather," Romy said, trying not to sound as shaky as they felt. They quietly made their way through the sea of mages to the imposing Centaur. "Commander Lustre?"

She looked down at him with tired and vicious eyes. "Name?"

"Romy."

"And your last name?"

"Technically, and legally, I do not have one. I'm a hedge."

"Does that mean you're easier to get along with than a coven mage?"

"It means that I won't ask you to fetch my lunch."

They couldn't tell if their answer satisfied her or not, as her face remained still as stone. "What do you want, Romy Hedge?"

"The green person over there," they pointed out a twitching, fidgeting Alfie, whose face was greener than it normally was. "He's an empath."

"So?"

"He's having issues controlling his powers right now. And empaths are able to manipulate emotions just as easily as they can sense them."

"So?" Her stony face continued to bedevil Romy's confidence.

"S-So…" Romy stuttered, but quickly regained their focus. "*Focuses*. Mages rely on maintaining emotional control in order to conjure their Focuses which keep their powers going. If he's in the room, he'll give everyone an anxiety attack and then nothing will get done."

"Ugh," she said with a sigh that almost sounded like a bray. "Fine. I'll have someone take him home." She pressed the call button on the walkie attached to her shoulder. "Acquati, front."

Romy's face fell. 'Oh no… By the fucking Heathen Gods.'

Within seconds, yet another face that Romy didn't want to see was in their line of sight. And an all too chillingly familiar voice rang through their ears. "Yes ma'am?"

Nicodemo Acquati. Nico. He/him. The shining star of MIST, and the very ex-boyfriend that had told Romy he was going to be moving to Chicago the night he broke up with them. A petite yet poised man, he looked even shorter next to the towering Lustre. His perfectly coifed ginger hair. His piercing sea-green eyes hidden behind thick, black-framed glasses that perfectly outlined his perfectly angular face. His freckles, like pebbles on a sandy beach along his perfectly poreless alabaster skin. His swirling conch shell necklace dangling over his defined chest. His uniform, snug tight around his taut physique. All were working hard to convince Romy that they were a fool for letting him walk out of their life. They had to make sure those feelings failed.

Nico refused to allow himself to even glance at his ex-lover of so many years. "How may I assist?"

"The little green man over by Al-Amin needs an escort. Take him home."

"Yes, ma'am," he said stiffly before turning on his boots and dashing over to Alfie.

"Is there anything else I can help you with?" Lustre asked in a stone-flesh tone.

"Yes, do you know where the bathroom is? I need to barf…"

"Really?"

4

Kill Your Darlings

"Hello," Governor Reynolds said. Her stoic and strong face was that of a woman in authority keeping control during her first cataclysm while running an entire state. "I want to thank you all for coming. I will not presume that I know anything about what's happening, which is why I invited you all here…"

Romy laughed quietly to themself. 'Invited is an interesting synonym for commanded…'

She went on with her speech about community strength and breaking barriers between the races, but Romy could not pay attention to any of it because their mind was split in five different directions.

'Why is Nico still here? Ugh… my sister is here too… I hope Guy's okay. I hope Alfie's okay. We need to get a fucking move on before my head explodes.' All these tangents were bouncing around in Romy's mind, threatening to completely unhinge it.

"Hedge!" A strong, deep, commanding voice called out.

"What?" Romy looked up and realized everyone was looking at them. "Oh, me?"

"Yes." Said Councilman Randall Proctor. The first mage to ever be elected to a political position in Massachusetts, and only one of a small few in the country. Like Romy, he was a hedge witch, and one of the most famous at that. Standing at about five and a half feet, his strong, handsome face and slightly greyed brown hair concealed an impressively powerful mage who'd renovated how the magical community viewed hedge witches. However, with his many accomplishments came an imposingly high bar for hedge witches to aspire to. "What is your name?"

Romy became flustered. 'What is my name? Wait… what is my name?"

"Sir hedge?" Proctor repeated.

Across the way, they saw Daciana sitting with her horde of vile-faced mage friends with a smile so wicked they were worried she would melt if it happened to rain.

After some brief internal struggle, Romy regained their composure. "I apologize for my absent-mindedness but I'm not a sir, sir."

"I apologize. What are your pronouns?"

They stumbled on how to respond to this question because it was a question they were, unfortunately, not used to hearing. "I am a Romy. I use they-them pronouns."

"Understood." He looked at his clipboard. "Romy, you are registered as a necromancer. You will work with the Ardelean Coven in investigating the source of the disturbance."

"No, he will not," they heard Daciana say as she stood up. "The hedge is a *former* member of the Ardelean coven and forsook his name in exchange for living in this city."

Proctor's eyes tightened on the witch and a look of irritation overtook his face. "The hedge, I believe, already announced *their* pronouns. Additionally, I was unaware, Miss Ardelean, that being a *hedge* disqualified one from being useful."

Daciana's tongue had suddenly been cut off. It was odd for Romy to see her show respect to a hedge mage. It was a humorously strange vision.

"Sir... I didn't mean to imply-"

"The meaning behind your words still have *implications* that are open to significantly less interpretation when you state outright that you are unwilling to work with a hedge witch, regardless of your relation to them."

Romy could swear they heard an "Oop!" in the deathly silent crowd coming from the door Kass was guarding.

"Yes, sir," was all Daciana could push out through her button lipped mouth.

He responded with a polite, "Thank you. Now, convene with Romy, the hedge. And do try to stay *professional*."

This time, there definitely was an "Oop!" And it was definitely Kass. The corner of Romy's eye caught Lustre shooting an intense look in her direction.

"All other mages will assist in research and development. If any of you have questions, direct them to either Commander Lustre or myself. Dismissed."

Looking over at their former coven, their hellhound death stares were screaming "no trespassing." They took a deep breath and made their way across the room. There were old faces – their cousins David, Iulia, and Claudia, their "Aunt" Bogdana's daughter, Sorina - and a few faces they didn't recognize. The Ardeleans had clearly gathered a larger following since they had left.

The lot of them did not say a word as Romy sat down.

Daciana cleared her throat to recover her voice after having it shoved down into her spleen. "This is what we know…"

Despite understanding the severity of the situation, being around their family caused Romy's mind to wander. Their thoughts fell back to the day they told their parents they would be leaving the coven to live as a hedge. Their father, Miron, did not challenge them. He did not scold them, or get angry, or yell. He just quietly recited the admonition.

"Go, hedge, and find no home in the Ardelean Coven, nor any other Coven in this world."

"Hedge!" Daciana yelled at them as someone threw a pencil at their head. "Are you paying attention? Finding it hard to focus? Hmmm?"

Romy squinted as they touched their hand to the impact site. "Excuse me, *Miss Ardelean*. I assumed since you were such a *qualified* mage you wouldn't need the assistance of a lowly hedge such as I."

The cold, uptight voice of one of the newer, younger Ardelean mages piped up. "Keep being cute, hedge. See what happens."

"Calm yourself, Raf."

Romy took this "Raf" in. No matter how hard they tried, they couldn't place him. He was in his early twenties at least. Mediterranean, either Italian or Greek, with glistening olive skin which made him stand out severely against the pale skinned, Romanian Ardeleans. He had bright hazel eyes and was wearing a hooded black cloak. Traditional garb for a coven necromancer, but incredibly inappropriate for the 90-degree Boston summer.

He spoke with the elegance and charm of a venomous snake. "We don't need a hedge tainting our circle."

Daciana rolled her eyes. "I think our *great leader* made his opinion on hedge operations very clear, so maybe we should just deal with it and try to move on."

Romy sat quietly as the coven rambled on about locator spells and tracking necro-magical signatures. These were all things they knew they all could do in their sleep. For a full hour, Romy sat still and silent. Nobody ever turned to them to ask for their opinion or input. Thus, they did not give it.

They all got up and started walking out of the room. Romy got up to follow but was stopped by Raf.

"This is a private Ardelean matter, hedge. You can stay here and help… the *second strings* catch up." And with a hissing laugh he slithered off to join the others as they exited the room.

Romy sighed with frustration.

They were ten years old again. Their sister, Daciana, was thirteen. Their little brother, Grigori, was eight. Their parents were always out of town on business, leaving them in the care of Bogdana, their mother's childhood best friend. She, as well as every other member of the coven, showed a clear preference towards Daciana. She was the golden child who frequently got away with murder.

But Romy still had their grandma.

On one particularly rough day, they found themselves running to her cottage on the outskirts of the territory.

"Bună! Bună!" They said, holding their burned hand, wrapped in the sleeve of their shirt, which had been ripped off in the scuffle.

As soon as she saw her grandchild, the wise, slouched, black clad witch's eyes widened. "What happened to you, my darling?" She ran as quickly as a seventy-five-year-old woman could and unwrapped their hand. "Oh, dear… Daciana up to her old tricks again, I see… Monstrous cretin."

"Bună!" They said, shocked mouth agape.

"What? Have you *met her*? Even as a baby, that hob-goblin would rip up my herb garden and spray the bats and crows while they slept." As she rambled, she pulled out several vials of herbs. Aloe. Witch Hazel. Lavender. English Ivy. And began mashing them up altogether with her mortar and pestle.

"Mom says it's bad to use language like that about my sister."

"Yeah, she told *you* not to call her names, but I can do whatever I want. And I say she's a jackass just waiting for the opportunity to buck someone in the back." Pulling out a small brush, she dipped it into the concoction and began spreading it over their wound. "She burned you, didn't she?"

They winced in pain. "It's fine. Mom told me not to bother her and I-"

"What? What did you do that would cause a sister to turn on her family so quickly? I told you - jackass waiting to buck. Now hold still." Romy froze in place. Her eyes began to glow a serene lavender as she activated her Hue and engaged her Focus. She began to rub the herbs into Romy's wound and her magic spread into their skin, mending it in seconds. "There we go."

"Thanks, Bună."

"Anytime, my love. Though, I do wish that we would see each other for less dire reasons… I can't count the times I've had to talk with your parents about that girl, but they're always on the move, bouncing from coast to coast doing Goddess knows what… Leaving you in the care of that crocodile. Ugh…"

"You don't like Aunt Bogdana?"

"That wretch? Goddess, no… And I do wish your mother would stop forcing you to call her that. She's *not* your aunt. She descended like a vulture the minute she found out your mother had married into our coven. Dropped her Florida swamp Coven and petitioned to join us barely a week later. Disrespectful… to forsake a name in order to patronize another… just… ugh! I hate her. I would have rejected her on the spot if I weren't so nice."

"You're the nicest, Bună," Romy said, sarcastically, with a twinkle in their eye.

She gave them a smart look. "Keep it up and I'll bake you into cutie pie cakes."

She started tickling them, resulting in a flurry of adorable giggle-cackles. "No! Not cakes!"

She allowed them to hide in the cottage until supper time. When nobody came for them, she didn't hesitate to start - figuratively - cursing their false aunt's name.

"What did I say? Swamp witch… you could get shot out of a cannon, but she'd still not take her eyes off your sister. *'She's the future of this coven! She'll light the way!'* She'll burn the forest down, that's what she'll do."

"Bună…" Romy asked, feeling smaller than they ever had before. "Am I useless?"

"Of course not! Have those idiots been calling you that?"

"I overheard Bogdana on the phone with my parents. She told them I was useless… cuz I can't activate my Focus. I have my Hue and everything but… I just haven't been able to… Daciana has been throwing fire since she was five. And Grigori is apparently getting closer to figuring his out and he's a billion years younger than me!" Romy started to cry.

"My darling, do you know how long it took me to learn my Focus?"

They sniffled. "How long?"

"It wasn't until I was a year older than you are now."

"What?! No, that's impossible."

"It is so possible. Have I ever lied to you, my love?"

"No…"

"No, I have not. Because I have no reason to do so. Those other children, and that Bogdana… ugh… they lie and hurt you because they can't see how special you are."

"I'm not special."

"You are so special, my dear. Trust me. You are like me. You are like my mother. You have spirit. And people who have spirit are constantly being put down by people that do not. You must stay strong when you stand against the winds of oppression. You will find your Focus, but only when you are ready to accept the power that comes with it."

After a bite of beef and noodles, night had descended on the Ardelean hollow, and it was time for Romy to brave the journey back to the hell that was home.

As soon as they opened the door, they could feel the heat of Daciana's taunting flames. "Well-well-well… little brother came crawling back after crying to grandma again? How adorable. Did you have fun with the old bag?"

In normal circumstances, Romy's chin would tuck into their chest, and they would simply walk away without saying anything. But they knew that not saying anything would not stop Daciana from hurting them. And they knew that she should not be allowed to get away with besmirching the name of not only their Bună but also their Coven's high mage. So, they made the decision to stand their ground. "Bună says you're a cretin who's jealous of my spirit because you're a terrible jackass."

Daciana's face scrunched up. "That old bag can't tell the difference between a spirit and a glow worm." Her bright violet Hue shined as violet flames erupted from her hands. "And me? Jealous of you?" She gave a sinister, arrogant laugh. "How can a wolf be jealous of the bones stuck between her teeth?"

From the darkest reaches of their mind, they felt a raging flood of feelings and thoughts course their way through their mind. And, without warning, formed as words they never thought they would have the strength to say. "I'm sorry. Bună was wrong. You're not a jackass. You're not a wolf either. You're just a sad, heartless little girl with nothing better to do than bully people weaker than you."

Having had enough of her younger sibling's sudden burst of resistance, she threw her fiery hand at their face with the intention of doing serious harm. But Romy would not burn this time.

Before she could react, Romy's eyes shined a brilliant magenta. They kept the powerful flood of strength and confidence fast in their mind and raised their hands against their sister's flaming fist. They started to produce a powerful, almost electric force. Surges and sparks flew about as a shield formed around Romy's hand. Both of the Ardelean siblings were shocked.

Daciana tried to regain her Focus, but Romy shattered it with their own as they concentrated even harder. They released a wave of powerful magical energy that threw their sister against the wall behind her. The shield had become a hand, holding her in place. And as they saw their cruel sister held tight under their magical grip, they figured it all out.

Their Focus was Confidence.

They released her and the hand dissipated. With a heavy thud, she fell to the floor. Exhausted from struggling beneath Romy's magical hold, she was too tired to fight back.

They felt strong. They felt light. They felt a headache form as they tried to keep ahold of that fleeting feeling that empowered them.

"I'm sorry," they said, sincerely. "I wasn't trying to hurt you. But I'll do it again if you make me."

Examining this memory, and remembering that child, they rediscovered that their greatest power is their Confidence. They had to remind themselves that their most powerful strength was their resolve against any oppressive force that attempts to impose over them.

They had no reason to bow to Daciana. And would not.

They had no reason to overthink Nico's decisions, as he is no longer a part of their life.

They had to focus all their effort and energy on the challenge that lay before them, and work hard to make sure things did not get worse.

A loud, screeching alarm blared through the room, shaking Romy to the core.

"Fucking what now?!" They said, out loud, without thinking.

The large doors opened up with a dramatic bang, and Nico re-entered the room.

"Acquati!" Lustre announced. "Report!"

Nico's frenzied and anxious state did not deter him from his duties. He gave Lustre a tall salute. "Commander Lustre. The dead are walking the earth."

Her mouth tightened. The lines around her eyes deepened. And after a frustrated delay, she let out a heavy, "Damnit."

5

Bodies in the Streets

The city had descended into total and utter chaos. Whatever chance the police and MIST had of safely evacuating the town had flown out the window as hundreds of zombies let themselves in the back door. And thousands of Bostonians ran in all directions in search of safety.

For Romy, zombies were old hat. Ripped from the Earth by magic with what little soul was left behind used to keep them together, they were mindless save for acting on the wishes of their master(s). In this instance, whoever was controlling these zombies clearly wanted the people of Boston terrified and/or dead.

The mages and MIST team attending the Conclave had been released to assist in managing the threat. As soon as they left the state house into the city streets, they were greeted by a sea of empty cars, abandoned in exchange for the comfort of the nearby shelter. Waiting for them, as well, was the pungent smell of corpses filling their noses. A lesser person would have gotten sick - like Kass was doing a few feet away - but Romy was used to it. And had a magical sigil that prevented nausea tattooed behind their right knee.

Councilman Proctor gave the call. "No collateral damage. No property damage. Your job is to seek, destroy, and defend. Advance!"

Kass's wings ripped out of her shoulders as she ran to Romy and lifted them up into the air. The Ardelean mages took flight on their broomsticks.

Romy pulled out their phone and dialed the first number that came to mind.

Straight to voicemail. "This is Alfie Pugh. Please leave me a detailed message containing your name, reason for calling, and a proper return phone number. Thank you."

Beep.

"Alfie, it's Romy, please call me or Kass back A-S-A-P. Let us know you're okay!" They hung up and started dialing Guy's number.

Straight to voicemail. "Hola, you've reached Guy! You could be texting me, y'know?"

Beep. They hung up before leaving a message.

"Fuck!"

"They'll be okay!"

"You're right."

The two did not have to fly much further before hearing a scream. A young woman was being chased by a flock of four putrid, rotting zombies. The sight hit the unfamiliar Kass like a ton of bricks, so much so that she nearly dropped Romy.

"Sorry!"

"Stay focused, queen. They're just dead people... That can move and bite and kill you."

Some were bags of flesh and organs barely clinging to exposed bone. Others were entirely skeletal, with only a hint of skin clinging to their decaying bodies. Their nails were gritted, rake-like talons, their hair was stringy and long, and their clothes were tattered rags.

Their Hue and Focus were prepped for this moment. Romy unleashed their "SoulSpark" - the name they gave their special power when they were younger. Surges and sparks of magical lightning radiated from their body as they threw pulses of force at the mindless horde. Two disintegrated immediately while the others were flung sideways.

Kass dropped Romy and rushed at the girl. "I'm gonna take her to the closest shelter. Text me if you need me."

Five zombies appeared and joined the two that failed to fall. "I'll be fine. It's just a bunch of walking corpses. Nothing new."

Kass flew off, leaving them to handle the zombies on their own. They summoned two volleyball sized bolts of energy in their hands and hurled them at the two struggling to make their way through the cars, reducing them to ash instantaneously.

The others closed in on them, but they stayed focused on keeping their confidence in the center of their mind. Thinking quickly, they began to run in the opposite direction of the nearest shelter. They sent intentionally low-level sparks in the direction of the zombies. Drawing their attention, they mindlessly followed as Romy led them astray.

Along the way, they saw several other members of the undead army attacking even more civilians. Throwing flurry after flurry of sparks, they pulled away each one until they corralled a great horde.

They turned a sharp corner into an alleyway and turned to face a dozen zombies. As soon as the militia of death filled the entire alley and seemingly backed Romy into a corner, they utilized the greatest benefit of SoulSpark: creating magical glyphs and sigils by bending the light produced by their Hue. These glyphs represented ritual symbols that conjured a variety of effects. Due to the extremely volatile nature of such magic, they had to be summoned with photographic precision. The wrong line in the wrong place could mean losing a foot, unless that was what the caster is hoping for.

They conjured five separate molecular acceleration glyphs on the ground beneath the zombies. And then the magic word. *"Detona."* In a flash, the sigils exploded, obliterating all of them in a single stroke.

A tap on their shoulder caused them to scream as high and as loud as possible. Kass, who had managed to land from above behind Romy without making a sound, screamed higher and louder in response.

"What the fuck is wrong with you? There is a zombie apocalypse movie playing out around us and you have the audacity to sneak up on me? I could've blown you to smithereens."

"Yeah, but you didn't, did you?"

"Doesn't mean I won't…"

"Okay bitch, good luck finding a new roommate in a dystopian world of the damned…"

They started to rub the bridge of their nose in annoyance. "Kass, do you need help with something?"

"I've already barfed twice in the past ten minutes. You wouldn't happen to have an antacid spell up your wizard's sleeve, would you?" Her keen senses had betrayed her. The very scent of death pervaded the air and turned her magnificent nose into a weapon against her.

"Maybe you should switch to shelter guard?"

Kass nearly retched. "Just help me."

They pressed their hand to her head. *"Goddess Panacea. Ill body and mind lay sentinel to waste. Strengthen her will and fasten her pace.*" Their magenta Hue stretched from their body and blanketed hers for a moment.

Her cat ears twitched. She gave a hefty sniff. The disgusting smell of corpses still cursed her, but she no longer felt the need to upchuck.

"You good?"

She gave a sweet smile. "Yes. Very. Thank you."

"You're welcome. Also, while you're here, why in all the Hells didn't you tell me Nico was still in town?"

Kass looked at them sideways. "Bitch, I didn't know until today. We don't see each other at work. And unlike someone I know, I don't google his name every day."

Their eyes tightened. "Bite me."

"I would but I'd have to get in line behind the zombies and Guy, wouldn't I?"

They grunted. "I feel like a zombie apocalypse is the wrong place to be making that kind of joke."

"You started it, queen…"

Without thinking, in their fury their Georgia accent came out. "Keep it goin', I'm gon' finish it." They were having a rough day.

Kass's head cocked to the side again. "Oooh, I'm pulling out the Georgia in you… or maybe it's the family reunion?"

Romy paused to collect themself. "Can we continue this conversation when the world isn't ending?" Suddenly a zombie appeared behind Kass. "Look out!"

She quickly spun, kicking, and slashing the creature in the face. The force of this hit sent it flying off to the side. "Are you kidding? I smelled him coming a mile away."

Despite the heavy impact, and the fact that it was already dead, it quickly regained its footing and charged at the two once more. This time, faster and more ferociously. Romy lifted their hand and disintegrated it with a wave of sparks.

"That's weird," they said.

"I mean… they're the living dead… of course they're weird," she said, aware she was pointing out the obvious.

"No, I meant they're getting faster. And more feral."

"Yeah. Zombies are supposed to be slow and basic, right?"

"Zombies are little more than attack dogs. They are never this organized or quick to recover." Giving it more thought, Romy had to point something out. "Why is my family here? What are a bunch of Podunk coven witches - *famous* coven witches, sure, but Podunk nonetheless - doing in New England of all places?"

"It is weird how they just happened to be here when all of this started."

"These zombies. The still incredibly red sky. It just reeks of the kind of magic only a necromancy coven like the Ardeleans can pull out of their pointed hats."

"And there are no covens like that living in Massachusetts?"

"If there were, do you think they'd be letting my sister run around town with her troop of circus clowns?"

"Fair point." And then she smelled something that stopped her dead in her tracks. "No…"

The two heard, and felt, a massive explosion that left a hard ringing in their ears. Kass was so struck by the sound that she fell to the ground. On reflex, Romy joined her.

"BOMB!" She screamed through the sharp tone blocking all other noises.

Romy put their hands against her ears and tried to regain their Focus. "*Cura!*" They shouted as their magenta Hue reached out.

Once again saved by her best friend's magical skills, the ringing dissipated and Kass was able to recover her composure. "Fuck this day."

"You're telling me? What just happened?"

"The Patriots lost." She could not help but joke. Overzealous humor was the two's conjoined coping mechanism. "A bomb just went off! C'mon." She grabbed Romy's hand and followed the smell of smoke and accelerant to the source. As she got closer, the fear swelled up inside her, clouding all other thoughts as she realized where she was going. "The shelter. Gods, no." A swelling of fear boiled inside her.

The final corner was turned, and they were greeted with the horrifying sight of the Myrtle Street Cataclysm Shelter and the Massachusetts State House completely ablaze. Flaming debris was littering the streets, alongside the bodies of several dozen unarmed civilians, mages, and MIST agents.

Romy looked on in horror. "There were hundreds of people in those buildings. The governor. Every hedge mage in the county. How could this happen?"

The answer to this question came in the form of a zombie running at them with a bomb strapped to its chest.

Acting on instinct, Romy reached out with their power and wrapped the creature in a constricting sheet of magical force a split second before it exploded. The blast pressed against their carefully crafted shield. The struggle to maintain their Focus, to stay confident that they could work this magic, was testing their resolve.

'It's okay. It's gonna be okay. Stay okay.' They kept repeating this in their mind as sweat formed on their forehead and their blood began to boil.

They realized they couldn't contain the blast much longer, so they had to think quickly. Looking up to the sky, vacant save for the hemoglobin-colored clouds, they threw the bubble upwards and released it. The sudden burst of heat, force, and light felled the two onto their backs.

As soon as she felt it was safe, Kass checked on her friend. "Are you okay?!"

"No." They struggled to get back onto their feet but forced themself to fight through the pain and strain. Their breath became heavy. The air was thick with smoke. "Survivors?"

"I don't know. I can't smell anything except fire and death..."

They fell to their knees. "I don't think I can cast right now."

"Don't push yourself. Just stay low. I'll scout."

She released her wings from their hiding spot inside her back and quickly flapped them about, pushing the clouds of smog away from them as she flew up into the sky.

Ignoring her advice, they forced themself up and started to look around through the haze. "Hello?! Is anyone there?!"

They saw someone struggle beneath a piece of rubble close to the blast zone. Despite barely being able to keep their legs from crumbling beneath them, they ran and threw the debris with what little strength they had. Beneath, they found the last person they thought they would see.

"Guy?!"

He coughed as he sat up. His eyes strained as he looked up. "Romy?"

"What are you doing here?"

They helped him up and started checking his body for any signs of injury. His already distressed denim jeans and worn out t-shirt were tattered and torn, but he had no cuts or bruises to speak of. His glasses were missing, but aside from that he was still the perfect angel Romy met the previous night.

He spoke through a throat sore from the smoke. "I was on my way outta town when a bunch of zombies started attacking everybody. I got out of my car and ran to the nearest shelter but then everything exploded. Do you know what's going on?"

Romy was floored by the happenstance of seeing their rebound in the field of battle. "This can't be a coincidence. The universe isn't this ridiculously serendipitous."

"What are you talking about?"

"Why are you at this specific location? Why this shelter?"

"This was the closest one to my car when the attacks started."

Romy could not believe it. Their mind began to speed up until it flew off the track. "No – no – There's something wrong with all of this."

"What do you mean?"

Their confusing conversation was interrupted by the guttural sounds made only by a creature devoid of breath and balance. Three victims of the bombing - a police officer and two civilians, each half burned - had risen. Zombies. Now poised and ready to kill.

Romy, confidence wavering, was unable to properly Focus. "Okay, you need to run." They grabbed Guy's hand and ran in the opposite direction.

Guy was shocked. "What?"

"Get out of here. Find Kass. She's flying around here somewhere. She has super hearing, just call out her name and she'll get you to the closest shelter. I can hold them off."

"You're worse off than me, I'm not leaving without you."

"This isn't a debate. They can kill both of us or one of us and at least I have a shot."

"Romy. No."

The zombies started running at them, much quicker than any undead Romy had seen before. They tried to summon their Focus, but their confidence was muddled by the thousands of thoughts raging through their mind.

'What is happening? People are dead. The dead are killing people. What does this all mean? Why Guy? Why here? Where's Kass? Where's Alfie? Where's Nico? Where's Daciana?'

"Romy, c'mon." Guy grabbed Romy's hand and pulled them away from the scene. He was like a firefighter lifting them from the rubble that was their mind. His courage pulled them out of their confusion. They spied a quiet alleyway, free of dead bodies walking or still.

"This way!" They pulled at Guy's hand and shoved him into the alley.

They ducked behind a dumpster. The heat of the summer made the dumpster untouchable, so the two had to sit uncomfortably without touching anything.

Guy decided to attempt to break the tension with humor. "So… do we make out now or what?"

"What?"

"That answers my question, I guess."

Romy left a pregnant pause before cutting it. "I'm sorry."

"For what?"

"For being weird earlier."

"It's okay. Given the circumstances, I think we're all allowed to be a little weird."

"Yeah, but there's just so much going on. It just doesn't make sense."

"The dead have risen and are exploding. Nothing makes sense anymore."

"Yeah. I'm still sorry."

"I forgive you… even though there's technically nothing to forgive you for."

Romy smiled. "Thanks."

"And despite the circumstances, I'm really happy we ran into each other."

"Why?"

"Cuz you ran off this morning before I could do this," Guy kissed Romy, but it wasn't the inferno it was before. It was a warm, comforting campfire. The kind of kiss that tells someone that everything is going to be okay. The kind of kiss that reinvigorates a person's faith in themself.

"Wow."

A series of rasping noises gave notice to the duo that a legion of zombies had arrived. Romy peaked out from behind the dumpster and saw at least a dozen zombies, hunched and slowly filling the alleyway.

"That's weird."

"The smell?"

"You are oddly comfortable right now, considering we might just die in a minute."

Guy shrugged what they just said off his shoulders. "We're not gonna die."

"Why do you say that?"

"Cuz I believe in you."

Suddenly, Romy felt the fire again. And a powerful burst of confidence. Their Focus ignited and their Hue lit up like Guy's sunshine smile. They lifted themself up and stood before the undead monsters. Summoning a massive glyph meant to disrupt a summoning, they threw it at the zombies who quickly turned to dust.

"Whoa!" Was all Guy could say.

However, it wasn't long before another throng of zombies closed in on the alleyway.

"More weirdness," they said to themself.

The zombies made a great run towards them. But before the creatures could attack, their heads were chopped off mid-run.

And then a familiar voice called out through the haze. "Romy? Are you okay?"

They squinted through the mirage of fire and mortar only to see: "Nico?"

He stepped forward, covered in dirt, cuts, and bruises but still very much alive. "Are you okay?"

A proper 'No,' was prepared but never made it past the tip of their tongue as the world faded to black.

6

Burn Notice

They did not fight. They did not argue. The weeks leading up to the inevitable break-up were spent exchanging breeze-soft words, with infrequent date nights composed entirely of silently watching television while eating take-out. Romy thought nothing of it. They were simply in a slump. In the end, though, they could not have been more wrong.

"I'm moving to Chicago," he said, a bag full of necessities packed and waiting by the door.

Romy, afraid of tears, refused to look him in the eyes. "When?"

"Two weeks…"

"When-" They choked up. "When were you gonna tell me?"

"I- I didn't know for sure until today."

They wanted to yell but could only muster a half-whisper. "Did I- did I do something?"

"No."

"Then why-" They fought back tears. They didn't cry. They hated crying. Crying in front of other people was something that only melodramatic attention seekers did. Romy did not want attention. They wanted to disappear. "Why?"

"It's just not working. Not anymore."

"What isn't working?"

"This. Us. Everything. I just-" He tried to find the best words. "I'm not going to pretend like I know what I'm doing. I don't know what I'm doing. All I know is that we're not as happy as we used to be. Things aren't the same. We're different people than we were nine years ago."

Nine years ago. They met while they were both studying magic at Harvard University's Beatrix Bishop College for Thaumaturgical Studies. Their eyes connected and it was instant fireworks. For Romy, they felt like they had been waiting for him their entire life. For Romy, they felt like they would be with him for their entire life.

Memories within memories danced in their mind as they tried to figure out where it all went wrong. To find the wrong in a sea of right and alright and okay.

"Did I do something?"

"No."

"Is it somebody else?"

"No."

"Then wha- what?"

"I just realized that I'm... I'm just not happy. Anymore. And I'm tired of not being happy. I want more. I want different. I'm... I'm sorry."

Romy didn't know what else to say. Their voice was gone. Their future was gone. They wanted to argue but couldn't. So, instead, they just said, "Okay."

He was stunned. "Okay? Romy, I-"

"Just go."

"Romy, I'm so sorry."

"Nico..." They stopped themself from saying anything that would expose the tears desperately trying to waterfall from their skull. "So am I."

And with that, Romy went back to their now half-empty room. They sat on the floor, back to the door, waiting to hear the front door slam. To their surprise, it took an hour before Nico eventually took his bags and left.

And then tears.

A knock at the door. "Romy? Sweetie? Are you okay?"

Kass was not scheduled to come home for another hour. Surely, Nico had called or texted to let her know what had happened and she knew she needed to check in. But Romy did not need a check in. They needed to comb through every moment in their relationship to decipher why Nico wasn't happy.

They tried to quickly relearn all the skills they had forgotten the moment Nico said goodbye. How to cope with loss. How to cope with disappointment. What it truly means to love someone other than yourself. What it truly means to love yourself.

And then, they could only ask themself one question. "What do I do now?"

But there was no right answer.

"I can't believe this." Kass. Frantic. Concerned. Scared. "What would she even want here? And you're sure it was her?"

"Positive." Alfie said in an emotionless monotone. A master at hiding his own emotions due to constantly being overwhelmed by everybody else's. "She was a massive concentration of self-afforded entitlement surrounded by a collection of weak-willed followers who each think they are all better than one another. It had to be Daciana."

"And she was searching for something?" Nico. Staying strong despite confusion, stress, fear, and internalized guilt.

"Yes, but she could not find it. She became very irritated, set our pet cactus on fire, then left."

Kass screamed. "NOT NICK JONAS!"

The shock sent Romy upright in their bed. "What?" Looking around, they saw that they were alone in their bedroom. Their quiet, ransacked, half-empty room. They were still in their clothes from before, but the minor injuries they had sustained had been healed. "Nico…" They could hear the others in the living room.

"What would she want here?" Kass asked.

"I mean, she's their sister, maybe she was looking for them to see if they were okay?"

'Guy? What's he doing here?' Romy got out of bed and walked to the door.

Nico responded. "Romy and their family aren't close in the slightest."

Kass continued. "Yeah… if she was here, it was def not for tea and cupcakes."

"Oh wow," was all Guy could say in the moment.

Nico turned to him. "By the way, who are you?"

"Guy Garrison," he said in a chipper voice, which was either dull to or completely dismissive of Nico's less than entertained attitude. "Nice to meet you."

Romy opened the door. "Guy?"

"Romy!" Kass was elated at seeing them up and awake. "Are you okay? Are you hurt at all?"

"No. I feel fine. Daciana was here?"

"Yes." Alfie said. "It was jarring. She broke the door down. She was with five other people. All of them dressed in black. I assumed they were mages. Also, I am happy you are feeling fine, Romy. I was worried."

They pulled him into a stiff hug. He gently patted Romy on the back. Alfie was not the best at public displays of affection, but he was getting better at it the longer he lived with Romy and Kass.

"I'm happy you're okay too, buddy." They turned to Guy. "Are you okay?"

Nico's face stiffened.

Guy's face was lined with worry and anxiety. "I have no idea, T-B-H."

Romy turned to Nico. "What are you doing here?"

"Why, yes Romy, I did heal your wounds. And it was very arduous. You're welcome. And, after I found your apartment partially on fire, I decided to help investigate."

Alfie added, "She is a very antagonistic woman. So much negative energy, an enthusiastic sense of superiority, and yet a sad tinge of jealousy, fear, and pain."

"Doesn't make up for the fact that she killed Nick Jonas…" Kass walked over to the incinerated cactus. "My poor pointy baby."

Nico continued. "She's one of the country's premier necromancers, and she decides to take time away from zombie hunting to loot her sibling's apartment. That's beyond suspicious."

Guy wanted to participate. "Suspicious A-F."

Nico rolled his eyes. "Maybe we should find a shelter for him until things blow over."

"I've tried literally every MIST radio frequency and emergency contact. They're all down. We have to assume the kami-zombies hit every other shelter in town."

Romy's head tilted in bewilderment. "Kami-what, sweetie?"

"Kami-zombies. Like kamikazes, but zombies. Kami-zombies. Okay, I've heard it out loud three times and have concluded that it was a bad idea. I'm sorry, but let's move on and focus on the bigger picture. Like it or not, Nico, Guy is gonna be safest here."

"While we're on the subject, what's the status of the zombies?" Romy asked.

"No major hits since the explosions," Nico explained. "I don't know if it's radio silence or what but there have been fewer and fewer reports of sightings since we brought you home. Back to the Guy, what if we have to leave? What's going to happen to him then?"

"We'll leave him with Alfie," Romy suggested. "Even if the zombies return, they aren't the best at going up stairs, and if Daciana comes back, she won't stand a chance."

Nico looked over at Alfie. "You're an empath, right?"

"Yes. I do not have many friends who are mages be-sides Romy as many find it uncomfortable that I am able to manipulate emotions. It is most often due to severe power-shift complexes."

"The point is: he can fuck up their Focuses and keep them from using their powers."

"More so than that, I can keep them from even noticing we are here. That is how I evaded detection earlier."

"Alfie," Romy asked. "I need you to show me everything you saw."

"Okay." He closed his eyes and conjured an illusion of himself.

"What is he doing?" Nico asked, only to be quickly shushed by Kass, Romy, and Guy.

"He's creating a projection of his memories," Guy explained. "He does it at work all the time. It's part of his regression therapy technique."

A great psychic force enveloped the room, producing an illusion of Alfie sitting on the couch nearby, watching the live news feed on television. Suddenly, the door exploded open with a quick burst of violet flame.

Daciana scrambled in; her face painted with disdain. "Spread out. Search every room, every cabinet, every drawer." She entered the living room and had a clear view of Alfie yet paid him no mind. She was followed by Raf, and all of Romy's other relations.

"Do you honestly think he'd be stupid enough to just leave it around?" Raf asked.

"Don't underestimate how stupid he can be."

Guy had to say something. "Misgender much?"

"That's her big thing. Invalidating my identity makes her feel like she has power over me."

Kass reared their attention back. "Guys, shut up and watch."

The Ardelean mages began ransacking the apartment, looking fervently for something they clearly could not find. Meanwhile, Daciana and Raf started rummaging through their bedrooms.

"I don't sense it," Raf said.

"It has to be here."

"Do you even know what it looks like?"

"What is this?" Kass said. "The pronoun game?"

Daciana became visibly upset. "Ugh!" She threw a violet fireball at Nick Jonas, leaving it to crumble into smithereens.

"You will be avenged, my sweet prickly friend," Kass said in a hushed tone. "Does anybody know how much I hate mysteries?"

Daciana continued to rage. "He must have it on him. We need to find him immediately."

"Do you think he might still be downtown?" Raf asked.

"If I know my little brother-"

"You do not..."

"He would be working to help all the injured peons. David?"

"Yes?" Romy's unibrowed cousin said.

"I need a locator spell."

"I don't know if that will be possible."

Her hands ignited, underlighting her face to make it look even more terrifying than it already was. "Make it possible."

"A lot of our Focus is being diverted to keep the summoning goin'. On top of that, with all the chaos, I can't guarantee a specific location."

"What can you guarantee, then?"

"Nothing. I can't guarantee anythin'. The best I can provide is a blood-to-blood tracker but considerin' all the blood relations they have in town their signature'll prob'ly get lost in the din."

"We stan a villain who respects pronouns," Kass said.

She growled. "FUUUCK! Let's just do a sweep downtown. I'll find Tooth and report in."

Something pinged in the back of Romy's mind. "Tooth?"

"That name sound familiar to you?" Nico asked.

"I don't know…"

The illusionary images of the Ardeleans dissipated as they left the apartment.

Alfie rejoined the group. "We know that they are downtown. We know that they are involved in the attacks. We know that they are channeling power to keep the spell going. And we know the name of an accomplice: Tooth. I do believe we are further along than we started."

Romy tried to concentrate. "Tooth... I can't quite place it, but I know I've heard that name before."

"Would you like assistance extracting the memory?" Alfie asked.

"Thank you, love, but I think right now having an empath in my head wouldn't be very helpful."

"Valid concern. I would not be able to ensure a pleasant experience."

"Moving on. The Ardeleans are scouring the city for me, I say we grab one of them and do a very friendly interrogation."

Kass added her two cents. "If we're electing witches to hunt down, I think we should go for that Raf brat."

"Really?" Nico asked. "Why him?"

"He's young, reckless, douchey, and his hubris is practically dripping out of his nose. He just screams 'I'm waiting to deliver a villainous monologue.' Also, I really don't like him." They all stared at her. "I promise not to torture him. I'm a good little kitty. Besides, if asking nicely doesn't work, we can get Alfie to check him out."

Romy followed her trail of thought. "He can disrupt his Focus and keep him from casting. But, if I'm being honest, we're probably better off with one of my cousins. Specifically, David. He's a mindless follower and his power is very passive."

"What can he do?" Kass asked.

"He can see hidden things… but, for some reason, not Alfie. Also, he can only use his powers when his eyes are closed."

"That's a manageable, and literal, blind spot."

"I mean, we can only hope that he hasn't become a better mage in the decade since I last saw him."

Nico's phone started ringing, instantly recognizing the number. "Commander Lustre? Are you okay?"

The commanding and terrifying voice on the other end could be heard throughout the entire room. "Where are you? I demand full details."

Nico gestured to the kitchen. "Kass, c'mon."

They went to talk with Lustre while the others continued. "Guy, if Alfie is coming with us then I'm gonna need to leave Kass here. Are you gonna be okay?"

"As okay as one can be in a zombie apocalypse."

"The world hasn't ended yet."

"And I'm sure it won't with you on the case." Guy's sunshine smile was slightly cloudy but still lit up the room. "I'll just stay here, shove every piece of furniture against the door, and wait for you to save everybody."

Romy swooned slightly. "I'll do my best."

Alfie could sense what was happening. "I am going to go to my bedroom to collect some provisions for the pursuit.

You both continue to explore your romantic and sexual feelings for one another."

Both sets of gay eyes widened without breaking contact.

"Thanks, sweetie."

"You are welcome," he said, before quickly ducking into his bedroom.

Romy's voice took a serious tone. "Seriously, though, are you gonna be okay? You've been through a lot today."

"Like the city being overrun with exploding zombies, having the person I hooked up with last night rescue me from being trapped under burning pieces of our state's capitol building and then that same person falling unconscious in front of me? Nah, it's all chill. Thankfully, I think all my childhood trauma is gonna cancel out any I get from this outstandingly bad day."

"Childhood trauma? Wow, we have so much in common."

"Yeah, I sensed that when your sister set fire to your cactus."

"Nick Jonas, you will be avenged!" Kass yelled from the kitchen.

"Yes, he will."

Guy gave Romy a brief but still electrifying kiss. "You can do this."

A flutter in their stomach. "You're distracting me. And I like it."

"Don't worry about me. I can take care of myself."

"And Kass'll take care of you too."

"No, I won't," she said, disappointedly, as she returned from the kitchen with Nico.

"All MIST agents have to report to the emergency command center in Seaport for role call and instructions."

"We told her about the Daciana situation, and Lustre refused to give us permission to allow a civilian - *Alfie* - to participate given all that's happened."

"I can't believe this. So, after a series of mass bombings, your commanding officer's plan is to gather everybody up in a confined area? She must be some sort of genius to come up with a plan as stupid as that."

Nico did not like that response. "She's stressed, operating with a skeleton crew, hundreds of people are dead, many of them government officials, and the zombies, after destroying half the city, magically disappeared and could reappear at any moment. Thus, action must be swift."

"And it's only going to get worse if we ignore this obvious lead."

"She gave us her orders."

"And they're *stupid orders*. Ignore them, or at least try and convince her that she's not thinking rationally."

Kass stepped in between them. "Okay, we are going to chill out *right now*. We have to go. Guy, I'm sorry but you have to come with us."

Nico's eyes rolled again.

Guy noticed. "What was that?"

"Nothing." He said in a flat monotone. "I am dedicated to my position as a protector of the people, peace and civility."

"Yeah, right, cuz you're *so civil*."

Nico closed his eyes and took a deep breath. "Let us escort him to the shelter and go from there. You should come with us too."

"I'm a mage, not a security lemming. And until I receive orders from whomever they've left in charge of the mages, I don't have to go anywhere."

Alfie decided to speak up. "Outside of that, regrouping is not a promising idea. And you both think so too."

Kass could barely contain her headache. "Alfie, please…"

"*We* are going to find David and question him," Romy said with an indignant face.

"We need to figure this out before something worse happens," Alfie said with calm resolution.

Nico was quite finished. "You couldn't handle yourself in the field for more than fifteen minutes and Alfie can't step outside without suffering empathic overload."

Alfie spoke to his defense. "I will admit I needed a moment to adjust, but I believe I can handle the stress of the situation well at this point in time. Particularly since the zombie issue appears to have been contained for the time being. Outside of that, as long as I am with them, Romy would not have to perform any large feats of magic."

"This isn't up for debate-"

Guy stood up to Nico. "You're right, this isn't. I don't answer to you, Nico."

Nico got in Guy's face, a considerable feat considering he was five inches shorter. "You're going to get yourself killed."

"Excuse me while I roll my eyes… oh wait, that's your job."

Nico turned away from him with a scoff. "Romy-"

"I said **no**. Besides… Don't you have somewhere to be?"

"Nico," Kass said as she grabbed Nico's arm. "They've made up their mind."

The two shared an intense, cold look that sent shivers up the spines of all in attendance. They never faltered as they wordlessly communicated their individual disappointment, shame, guilt, and grief in a single instant.

Finally, it was Romy who broke the foggy silence. "Let's go, Alfie."

"You are very upset. Are you sure you wish to leave now?"

"*Let's go, Alfie.*"

Nico did not say a thing as he watched them leave the apartment.

'I guess it's my turn to leave you speechless,' They thought.

7

The Calm During the Storm

The Seaport Cataclysm Shelter had been transformed into a triage center, as well as the emergency MIST headquarters. It rested safely in a magically reinforced bubble beneath the bay near the Seaport World Trade Center. The bubble provided a very scenic view of the underwater world, which was meant to have a calming effect during the worst of times. However, the terrible sky turned this once picturesque vista into a hideous red reminder of the day's circumstances.

Whatever glimmers of hope Kass and Nico held in their minds before arriving were quickly smothered by what they were facing. Medical tents had been erected in every spot on the ground that did not have a flat bed, while a care center for lost or abandoned children sat in the corner. All they could hear were the cries of infants, calling out for their lost parents. The din was so thick that they could barely hear their commanding officer, Lustre, standing right in front of them.

"COME THIS WAY!" She shouted, leading them to a private conference room.

Kass looked over at Guy, and he looked twice as shell shocked as they did. Knowing she could not tell him "Everything will be okay," she grabbed his hand and softly stroked it.

He looked up at her, smiled, and then walked over to the nearest triage station, and grabbed the attention of a Satyr medic carrying a mass of bandages on a silver tray. "Does anybody have a guitar?"

"What?" The bewildered Satyr responded as they bandaged a bleeding arm wound.

"Never mind. I'm sorry."

As Guy turned away, the medic gave him a look. "Weirdo…"

Guy looked around, hoping to find something he could use to help the only way he knew how. A tap on his shoulder alerted him to the return of a plain-faced Nico.

"You see that pile of junk over there?" He asked, pointing to a collection of wood, plastic, and wire left behind from a broken bunk nearby.

"Yeah?"

"Bring it over here."

"Why?"

"You said you needed a guitar."

Guy quickly jogged over to the pile and brought it to Nico. He activated his Hue and began glowing an icy blue. And, in a perfect Italian accent, he cast his spell.

"*Musica. Apollo. Construire. Efesto. Saggezza. Atena. Chitarra.*" Right before Guy's astounded eyes, Nico's ice blue magic pulled the bits and pieces together to build a patchwork guitar. Strings and all. "You'll have to excuse the tuning. I'm not the best at… music stuff."

Guy gleefully held it in his hands and gave it a light strum, producing a hideous harmony. "It's okay. I can work with this. Thank you!"

"You're welcome," he said, flatly, before turning around.

Guy wanted to ask, "Hey, why did you do that?" But he was already certain it was his way of saying "sorry for treating you like shit because you fucked my ex."

He did not have magical powers. All he had was a well-meaning heart, an open mind, a kind ear, perfect pitch, and the ability to play any instrument one could name thanks to the kind of musical education only an incredible amount of privilege could pay for. And he was intent on using all these skills to help everybody around him.

After quickly tuning his new instrument, he walked over to the cluster of inconsolable children, all red-faced and teary-eyed from fear and loneliness. Just the presence of Guy's kindness, the heart and smile that shined like the sun, was enough to calm some of them down.

"Hey guys, I know that everything that's happened today has been really scary. I'm scared too. I was kinda hopin' me and my buddy here could maybe play some music for you? If that's okay?"

One of the children said, "Yes, please," which melted Guy's heart.

"Alright, how about I strum a few chords and see how we all feel after? Hm?"

He started to play a soft, lullaby melody. A sweet and warm tune that echoed through the room. All fell silent as he began to sing a simple "la-la-la" with his rich tenor. His music captured the heart and soul of all, easing their trauma ever so slightly, helping them forget their woes.

A less than entertained nurse whispered, "He needs to stop. That music could be a distraction for the medics."

However, the attending medic hushed them. "No. It's helping. It's really helping."

"Acquati," Lustre said in a commanding, annoyed tone as Nico entered the conference room. "I'm so happy you could join us. We were just about to go over casualties, fatalities, the fact that the mayor, five out of thirteen city councilmembers, and a good chunk of the house of representatives are all dead or missing. And, of course, the newly acquired information that your ex-partner's family appears to have been *behind it all*."

Nico was stunned. "Uh."

Lustre ignored him and continued. "Oh, and please, let me introduce you to all that's left of Boston MIST."

She gestured around to the few dozen uniformed guards filling the room.

"Oh, my Gods…" Nico said under his breath.

Looking around, he saw Kass holding back tears as she put on a brave face. He wanted to go to her, to comfort her like the friend he used to be, but he needed to keep his position by the door.

"We were a score of hundreds. The bravest and the brightest. And the Ardelean Coven took advantage of our creed to protect the innocent at all cost… and we paid the ultimate price." With her head held high despite the immense gravity of the situation pushing the weight on her shoulders down to the floor, Lustre took command. "What do we know?"

Nico spoke for the group, "The Ardeleans have used what is likely an incredibly large summoning sigil in tandem with incredibly coordinated cooperative magic to create an army of zombies."

A wood nymph decided to add her piece, "Every cemetery in the county is, forgive my phrasing, bone dry."

Kass also contributed, "And whenever a zombie adds another body to the death toll, another one rises."

"But they've stopped," Lustre said. "Do we have any clue as to why?"

Nico pondered for a moment. "It's been quiet for a long time. My only assumption is that the cooperative magic needed for the summoning must be incredibly taxing on all of them. So, they must need to recharge every few hours to keep from draining themselves."

"Well," Lustre resumed, "that gives us some time for a much-needed reprieve. We must use this time to regroup and think of a counter strategy. Perhaps try and find one of the coven mages and get them to talk."

"We should also think of a contingency plan in case this base gets compromised," Nico said.

"What do you have in mind?" Kass asked.

"The Wizard Gerhardt's Mass Translocation Spell."

"Acquati," Lustre addressed him. "Do you think you could pull it off?"

"Very much so. But it requires a lot of cooperative magic. I'd need another mage."

Kass asked, "Ma'am? Are there any mages left that aren't with the Ardeleans?"

Lustre sighed. "An overwhelming percentage of the county's registered hedge witches were among the first reported casualties. Nothing has been confirmed, but there's reason to believe that neither zombie nor bombing had anything to do with their deaths."

"Oh, Gods," Kass swore under her breath. "It had to have been them. Daciana, and the others. They came here to cast this spell, to steal something from Romy."

"Steal what?" Lustre asked.

"We don't know yet. But we do know that it's powerful and they need it for whatever they're planning."

Nico felt it was his turn to speak. "And Tooth. There is an informant, or an accomplice they referred to as Tooth."

Lustre scratched her head and whipped her big tail. "Well, it's a lead. It may not be a lot but it's a lead. We need to find the Ardelean mages."

"Romy is already on it."

Lustre looked at Kass with wide eyes. "Could you repeat that?"

As her commanding officer towered over her, her confidence imploded. "Romy, the hedge mage, has already started looking for someone to interrogate."

"Romy, the hedge mage, whose family may be behind the greatest cataclysm since the Witch Wars, is wandering the streets alone when they should be here, in the safety and security of this building?"

Nico jumped in. "Ma'am, we didn't have a choice."

"What do you mean, you didn't have a choice?"

"Romy refused to come with us. We couldn't force them."

Kass jumped in. "They were going to find one of their cousins. They believe they might be able to get him to talk. Alfie, the empath, went with them."

Lustre sighed and started rubbing her forehead. "Well then, Romy has made themself priority number three. Priority number one: protecting this shelter. Priority number two: maintain constant radio vigilance. We need to know if there are any other shelters, MIST operatives, mages, and civilians still alive out there."

Kass stepped forward. "Commander."

"Yes, Al-Amin?" Her tone gave away how heavy the recent events had fallen on her shoulders.

"I wish to lead the priority three mission, ma'am. I live with Romy and Alfie. I could trail their scents, fly out and get them back here in minutes."

"Granted. But we're operating on a skeleton crew, so you'll be going alone."

"Understood," she said, spine straightened, ready to bear the burden. She not only wanted to prove to Lustre that she should have faith in her, but she also wanted to show her that she wasn't alone.

A quiet smile on the commander's face showed her that it had worked.

"Please, let me go with her," Nico said.

Kass shot him a look as Lustre balked. "Did you not hear a word I just said?"

"But if they get attacked by mages-"

"Acquati, look around. I shouldn't have to explain to you why your skills here would be *invaluable*. You stay."

Nico's face turned to a stone as he accepted his position. "Yes, ma'am."

Guy had started moving about the room, spreading his beautiful music to all. Improvising melody after melody, calming the doctors, the nurses, the patients, and the guards. Bringing them a glimmer of peace. Of hope. For even in their darkest hour, they had his music, and that was what was going to get them through the night.

As he wandered, a bandaged hand reached out to him. "Please, young man. May I ask a request?"

"Consider me your own private jukebox," he said with that sunshine smile. Guy knelt down to get a better look at him. Half of his body was badly burnt, covered in tattered and poorly applied bandages.

"Do you know *Ardóimid?*"

Guy had to think for a moment. "That's an old Irish folk song, isn't it?"

"Yes... it's been passed down through my family for generations. I sang it to my daughters. I sang it to my wife."

"Hold on, sir." Guy pulled out his phone and searched for the song, finally coming up with a series of chords. "D-flat major. No sweat. Forgive my terrible Irish accent."

The man chuckled, then coughed.

Guy smiled, hoping it would bring comfort. And then, as he began to strum those gentle strums, he lifted the man's spirits with his soft but powerful voice.

"We hear it with the light of dawn, Ardóimid. Ardóimid. For every daughter and every son, Ardóimid. Ardóimid. Be not afraid of the shadows of the night. They are your keepers. They are your light. Be not afraid of their torches and stakes. For fire will ne'er belong to they. So, sing it when the moon is high, Ardóimid. Ardóimid. So, sing it when the end is nigh, Ardóimid Ardóimid."

The man smiled and coughed. "Even with those butchered, Americanized lyrics, it still rings a sweet bell in my cold heart."

It took a moment for Guy to realize it, but he recognized the man. "You. You're Councilman Proctor."

He cough-laughed again. "Yeah… some mage I am? Couldn't even stop myself from exploding."

"Hey, you'll get through this. They have amazing doctors and healers."

"I appreciate your candor, Guy, but don't hold out hope when its better spent on those who can still feel their toes." He cough-laughed.

"Hey, toes are over-rated, I-M-H-O."

"Says someone who probably still has ten."

He smiled softly. "Let me play you another-" Then a thought struck his mind. "How did you know my name?"

"I'm a politician, young man. I know everything."

Guy did not want to let on how uncomfortable he was, so he continued smiling and playing as he got up. "Well, it was nice talkin' to ya. I hope you feel better soon."

"Of course, I will, young man. Flesh wounds are nothing compared to a knife to the soul."

This froze Guy in his tracks. He turned back to try and get a good look at the half-burned, bandaged man. "Have we met be-"

But his sentence was cut off by a blood-curdling scream. "AAAAAAAAAIIIIIEEEEEEEE!"

Guy turned towards the source, only to see a massive flood of water fill the room, and a great piece of glass fly towards him.

Nico watched as Kass flew out of the shelter. He was supposed to be in Chicago, watching the carnage unfold from the safety of his new desk. But then, out of nowhere, every file and form he had filled out for the transfer disappeared into thin air, forcing him to refile. Then his mental competency hearing was rescheduled three times before he was inevitably declared capable of handling the stress of moving to a different time zone. And then he had to re-register his mage's license to accommodate travel just in case he had to use magic while on the airplane. And that led to him applying for magical flight insurance, which required a dental mold for reasons he couldn't fathom.

As a result, he had been forced to stay at an incredibly uncomfortable hostel while most of his belongings were already at his new apartment. And now he was forced to fight through a terrible cataclysm alongside the ex-partner he dumped to go live in Chicago. The ex-partner who left their coven to be with him. The ex-partner who supported him through his transition, long before they ever started dating. The ex-partner for whom he still had incredibly complex feeling.

"I'm an asshole," he said to himself.

A blood curdling scream. "AAAAAAIIIIIIIIEE-EEE!"

He ran to the inner sanctum of the shelter just in time to watch a great flood burst through the now broken glass wall. Acting on instinct, Nico mentally took hold of the wave and stopped it from filling the room. With his powerful control over all forms of water, he pushed it back out into the bay and froze the hole closed. A few people cheered and clapped, while others groaned in pain as the water had irritated their injuries.

"Is everyone okay?" He asked the room.

"This man needs help, right now!" A young triage nurse announced.

Nico ran over to him, only to discover that the man in need was Guy. A great shard of glass had pierced his chest. His mouth was gushing blood. He was going into shock.

"Oh Gods. What happened?"

"A massive piece of glass just flew out at him."

"Is anybody else hurt?" He looked around, but nobody else appeared to have been affected by the break. In fact, if it weren't for the puddles of leftover bay water littering the floor, he wouldn't have been able to tell that the wall even broke. No shards. No glass. No trace.

"No, it's just him. Do you know any curing spells?"

"Of course, but we're going to need to pull it out of him."

"But if we do that, he might hemorrhage."

"I can manipulate the flow of his blood using my powers. You just have to hold him back."

The two worked together. The nurse held onto Guy's body while whispering, "It's gonna be okay, sweetie. You're gonna be okay. Just hold on."

Meanwhile, Nico used all of his strength to pull the blade of glass out, dropping it to the floor with a heavy thud.

"Okay, now I just need to-"

But no magic was needed. As soon as the shard had been removed, a flourish of blood red energy emerged from inside him. The gaping wound in his chest closed up in an instant. The flow of blood coming from his mouth ceased. His body regenerated itself as he drifted off into a comfortable unconsciousness.

"Wow," the nurse said. "That was amazing."

"That... wasn't me... I don't know what that was."

8

Dead is a Four-Letter-Word

The streets were as dead as the occasional body Alfie and Romy stumbled across. The sky was still a devilish red, radiating its ever-growing necro-magical force. Yet the corpses maintained their lifelessness, as if refusing to be turned into zombies. Meanwhile, national news sources were reporting the casualties in the hundreds as more and more were reported dead, injured, or missing each minute.

Romy was leading Alfie downtown toward their target, David, holding their phone out with the maps app open. A small dot produced by a powerful tracking spell divined his location and granted them the upper hand.

"Gotta love modern day scrying. Yay technology." Romy was trying to come off as unbothered. However, something weighed heavy on their mind. And, as a result, it weighed heavy on Alfie's as well.

"Are you okay?"

"You already know the answer, so why ask?"

"Because you need to talk about it."

"We *need* to find my cousin."

"We can do that and talk about your feelings."

"I'm aware."

"So, what is stopping you?"

"Because I don't want to."

"But you should."

"Alfie!"

"Okay." And with that, he receded.

The dot on the map disappeared. "Alfie, wait."

Alfie sighed. "Must you do this, every time?"

"I'm sorry, really, but this is the only way to properly engage a tracking spell with all that's going on."

They handed the phone to Alfie and ripped off the bandage they placed over the small flesh wound they had made on their right index finger only moments earlier. With just a small push, blood began to trickle out again, which they pressed onto the phone to leave a bloody fingerprint, which dissolved into the magic of their Hue. Thinking of David, they cast their spell. *"Heart to heart. Mind to mind. Blood to blood. Soul to find."* The dot representing David reappeared. "Wonderful."

"Magic can be very disgusting."

"You should see the shit I have to do to perform a seance."

"I would rather not see any kind of feces, thank you."

They continued on their way. The downtown area was still yet another half hour before them.

A solid ten minutes passed without either saying a word.

Inevitably, it was Romy who broke the silence by trying to lift the anvil sitting on their heart. "I miss him."

Alfie automatically went into therapy mode. "That is understandable."

"Is it? He broke my heart. Why would any intelligent person want someone like that?"

"You were together for many years. What did you think you would feel when you saw him again so soon after you ended the relationship?"

"Pissed off... And I was... for a minute. When I saw him there, in the living room we used to share. When I felt the scars he left after he healed me while I was asleep. When I saw the way he was treating Guy. I wanted to yell at him at the top of my lungs until I knew I could never cast again."

"And yet you did not, why?"

"Well, I was a tad busy being overwhelmed with everything else going on."

"But when you were not overwhelmed? When you took charge and regained your confidence? Why not?"

"I was trying to comprehend my family's culpability in a mass murder."

"Romy…"

"I don't want to talk about it. We need to focus."

"Then when do you think would be an appropriate time to do so? Before or after we are all dead?"

"Ugh… Fuck you."

"Stop avoiding your feelings, Romy. Why do you miss Nico?"

"Because…" They didn't want to admit what they knew they had to let out. It struggled behind their lips like a trickle of water ready to demolish a great dam. And then, the floodwaters. "I still love him."

"Are you ashamed of that?"

"Yes."

"Why?"

"Because he dumped me, Alfie."

"Is that supposed to negate your feelings?"

"It's supposed to make me angry."

"Why?"

"Because when people leave you, it hurts."

"And being abandoned makes you angry?"

Romy rolled their eyes. "A lot of things make me angry, Alfie."

"What else fills you with as many complicated emotions as you are feeling right now?"

Romy sighed. "Fuck you."

"I know you do not mean that, but it is an avoidance measure, and I would rather not talk at all if you intended on evading your own feelings and the issue at hand."

"Ugh!" They hated how hurt they felt. They hated it so much that they stopped walking to kick the ground and jump around like a toddler. "I miss my family! I hate them. I love them. They're monsters. They're murderers. They raised me. And they've treated me like nothing ever since I left, but I'm the one that *left them*! I left them because they made my childhood a living hell! But I still want them to love me! I still want their approval and their kindness and their respect, even though I know I'm never gonna get it. Why? What the fuck is wrong with me? Please. Please, dig deep into my brain and just explain it to me before I explode along with the rest of the world."

Alfie allowed a long, pregnant pause so that Romy could catch their breath. He could feel every ounce of pain and strife stampeding through their heart. It almost drowned them both. But Alfie had to be the life jacket.

"I could. I could fix everything for you. But then what would you learn? We both know that magic - and being psychic - creates an ease of access into solving problems, but it completely subtracts the work that needs to go into making sure those problems do not resurface."

Romy started to cry and hated themself for it. "Fuck."

"Do you think Nico hates you?"

"I know Nico doesn't feel the way he used to feel about me. I know that Nico left. I know that Nico doesn't want to be with me anymore. So, I shouldn't love him anymore, right?"

"There are no expectations of you. You feel what you feel, and you want what you want. I will impart no judgment nor the cruelty of an opinion that dismisses what you are going through."

"Ugh… Fuck this day… Fuck this day with a chainsaw covered in sandpaper dildos."

The scarlet sky had turned a blood red-tinted black as day turned to night and the two finally made it downtown. The blip drew them to a small alleyway in Dorchester. As they hid behind a collection of dumpsters, Alfie maintained a watchful third eye, his antennae stiff and upright as they continued to glow in the darkness.

"Small mind. Low confidence. Miniscule amount of willpower. Insecure about his status in the hierarchy of his community, lost without direction… You were right, he is the perfect candidate for interrogation."

"Yeah," they said, with a hesitantly sympathetic sigh. "David always was the… you know."

"Pushover. Indeed. He thinks so too. There are decades of severe bullying just belaboring his mind beyond reason.

It is a wonder that he is able to tie his shoes in the morning without breaking down in tears."

"I wouldn't put it past him. Can you get a good lock on him?"

"Yes."

"Where is he?"

Alfie pointed to an abandoned bar across the street, its window shattered from what must have been a terrifying melee. "In there. In the bathroom. Let us, at least, give him the dignity of finishing before we tackle him, shall we?"

"Of course. I'm not a monster. Unlike some people in my family."

"And be gentle. His heart aches with so many conflicting emotions, but mostly pain and regret."

"I will do what I need to do to protect us and get what I came for. Be the good cop if you want, but he's still complicit in the murder of hundreds, regardless of how sad he is."

"Understood, but my nature draws me towards sympathy for those who commit atrocities as a result of abuse."

"Abuse isn't an excuse."

"I am aware, it is but an explanation. Yet, let us try my approach and go forward with a kind foot."

"Ugh. Fine. By the Heathen Gods, you're worse than…"

Alfie's antennae perked. "Calm down. He comes."

They watched as David quickly ran out of the bar, zipping up his pants as he tripped over his own feet. He was a slightly older, visibly depressed, baggy-eyed, unibrowed, greying version of Romy. A dark look into an alternate reality where they had stayed with their coven.

"Be gentle," Alfie warned. "He is very fragile. All of this is weighing heavy on his soul."

"I know how to talk to my family, even if it's been forever." Romy rushed towards him. "David."

David turned, his gaunt face giving a comically shocked expression as his eyes almost bugged out of his head. Too smart to face Romy in battle, he simply ran the other way. However, Romy quickly activated their Hue and used it to move a car to block his path. He tried to activate his own but found it impossible.

"Please! Don't hurt me!" He said, with a strained Georgia accent. Speaking as if constantly working out a gastrointestinal issue.

Romy ran up to him. "I don't wanna hurt you, David. But if you attack me, or my friend, I won't have any choice."

Alfie stepped forward. "Hello, David. I am Alfie."

He looked him up and down. "What are you?"

Alfie, like a true professional, used to hearing that annoying question, ignored it entirely. "That is not important. What is important is how you feel right now."

"What are you talkin' bout?"

"David," Romy said. "Please, tell me, what is Daciana planning? Why are you here?"

David struggled. The tension in his brain was visible to all. "It doesn't matter."

"Why does it not matter, David?" Alfie asked.

"It's too late. Way too late. We can't stop him."

"You mean Tooth?" Romy asked. "Who is he?"

"I can't tell you."

"Yes, you can, David." Eventually, Romy's own southern accent started phasing back in. "We both know that what you're doin' – what you've done – is wrong."

"You need to go." He tried to turn away, but they grabbed his arm and pulled him back.

"Why, David?"

The more they said his name, the more pain he showed in his face. "I can't tell you."

"Why can't you tell me?"

"The Covenant."

Romy's eyes widened. "David-" They shook their cousin. "David, why would you do that?!"

"You know I can't tell you. So, stop askin'. All that matters is that if you don't turn yourself over to Daciana, more death will come."

"And if I do, then what will happen?"

David's heavy, dark eyes pierced through to Romy's soul. "The end of everything else."

They realized that he could not be helped. "Go."

Alfie realized it too. "We will run."

David nodded. "I really am sorry."

"It doesn't matter anymore, does it? You've made your bed. And everybody else's coffin."

A tear welled in David's eyes as he turned and ran away, leaving Alfie to wonder.

"What is a Covenant? I know that, to an ordinary person, it would mean a legal agreement, but what does it mean to a mage?"

Romy started walking away from the scene, with Alfie trailing close behind. "It's a magical pact. A contract that binds you mind, body, and soul to fulfill the terms under penalty of death. He's sold his soul. And we need to get as far away from here as possible. If every Ardelean, every conspirator in Boston is under a Covenant then they'll stop at nothing to get what they want. Because their lives literally depend on it."

"But we do not know what they want."

"And, as demonstrated, they can't tell us anyway. So, we're gonna have to figure it out ourselves, won't we?"

"They came to our home. They thought you kept it there. What would it be? A tome? A spell? A potion?"

"I don't have anything they don't already have, and I don't know anything they don't already know."

"But it is something that only you can offer."

"And it's important enough to justify murdering an entire city of people."

"They needed an excuse to get you out of your apartment."

"It's something that could only be taken by force. They think it's precious?"

"Why are you asking me?"

Romy stopped dead in their tracks and cursed at the sky. "Because I have no fucking idea what's going on. I'm lost. I'm confused. I'm in a lot of pain, and I am damaged." Romy slumped and fell onto the dirty, rubble covered street and looked upwards. "I miss the moon. It's supposed to be a source of power and a guide to a lost witch. And I have never been more lost."

Alfie laid down on the ground next to them. "You are not lost. The road ahead is foggy and unclear, but you can make it through. We are on the right track; we are just missing several key facts about the situation."

"So then let's evaluate: one - my sister and several other necromancers came to Boston to summon zombies and kill everybody."

"Two - during the chaos, your sister ransacked our home in search of something important."

"Three - they've all been cursed to not speak of this plan to anybody."

Just then, a thought came to Alfie's mind. "I believe I have an idea of what they're looking for."

Romy looked puzzled. "Really?"

"Yes. But there is a problem."

"What?"

"We are surrounded."

"What?!" Romy sharply leapt up onto their feet and looked around.

As Alfie said, they were indeed surrounded. A gang of pale-faced youths, all with a hint of bloodlust painting their faces, had closed in on them while they allowed themselves to be distracted.

"Well, this is exciting." The ringleader stepped forward. A young man practically oozing pompousness with stance and carriage. No older than seventeen, with perfectly coifed, bright blond hair, dressed in a fashionable black, pin-striped suit, worth at least several hundred dollars. But what stood out the most to Romy were his blood-red eyes, with black sclera.

"Vampires…" Romy whispered.

"I am fully aware what they are," Alfie responded, his voice suddenly heavy with pain.

"Alfie?" The leader smiled smugly, exposing his fatal fangs. His accent was a muddied Welsh, not unlike Alfie's. "What a pleasant surprise."

"Ianto."

"You know him?"

"He more than just 'knows' me, fair mage. Oh, this is delicious."

Romy pulled their friend close to their side for safety. "Alfie?"

"He is my brother."

The flock of blood-sucking fiends all laughed, callously.

Romy had had enough with the strange, serendipitous nature of the day's events. "What the Hells is going on here? Is it family reunion apocalypse day, and nobody told me?"

"You'll be coming with us, loves." Ianto signaled for his underlings to close in. "No use trying to escape. You are outclassed, outnumbered, outgunned, and we have your scent."

The group all withdrew an overkill amount of military grade firearms and aimed them straight for the two.

Vampires were humans, sired through a blood exchange. Victims of a disease that trapped them between the mortal world and the hereafter. As a result, they could not use magic nor could magic be used on them. They had great strength, and were intelligent hunters, capable of using their bloodlust-driven cunning and charisma to lure innocent victims to their doom. Despite their power, they still had several standard weaknesses, which Romy was clever enough to capitalize on.

They activated their Hue and summoned a great sigil with the light of their SoulSpark. *"Lux!"*

The air around them erupted in a blinding flash, mimicking the intensity of the sun well enough to send the flock running for fear of bursting into flames. When the flash dissolved, Romy and Alfie had vanished.

"Find them!" Ianto ordered, and with that his servants ran, following the trail of their delicious aromas.

However, for as clever as a vampire could be, none of them thought to look up. If they had, they would have found Kass holding them aloft, her wings flapping the wind about. Their scent blown about the breeze.

"I want you both to remember this moment the next time you wonder whose turn it is to do the dishes."

9

Six Feet Overwhelmed

The air in the conference room of the Seaport Cataclysm Shelter was so thick, one would need a chainsaw to properly pierce it. Kass, Alfie, Nico, Lustre, and Romy sat together at a round table while two MIST agents - a Minotaur and a Kobold - watched the open door.

Commander Lustre stood up on all four of her legs and began to pace about the room. Her once perfectly slicked back ponytail had become undone. Great bags big enough for a transatlantic flight's worth of luggage formed under her eyes. She was beyond traumatized but pressed on like the champion she knew she had to be. "Obviously, none of this is coincidence."

"Understatement of the millennium," Romy said under their breath as they rested their tired legs on the chair next to them.

"We have a murderous cult employing vampires, zombies, and Gods know what else to find *you*," She pointed her sharp nose at Romy. "Searching for something *you* have. Something *we* can't even interrogate *them* about because of a curse that keeps them from giving out any information. And one such vampire - the leader of the pack it seems - just so happens to be the brother of your roommate."

"Adoptive brother." Alfie felt the need to point it out. "But brother, nonetheless. Continue. Excuse me."

She stared at him with tired, yet still penetrating eyes. "And then, of course, we have our lovely Mister Garrison. A seemingly ordinary man. Who, in a freak water break accident which harmed *absolutely no one else*, suffered an injury that would have instantly killed any other person on the planet... yet still he stands?" She sighed and rubbed the bridge of her nose. "I don't think it needs to be said but I'll say it anyway: we are completely and utterly screwed. I have several dozen wounded here. MIST agents are reporting in, sporadically, from all over the city. The whole city is in chaos and ruin. And to top it all off we may be looking at Witch Wars Two."

Romy's eyes began to water. "Witch Wars Two..."

"Hedge... I mean..." She caught herself. "Romy... Please, if you know anything, I invite you to share until your mouth gets tired."

Romy refused to cry. "Excuse me while I go grab my diary so I can fill you in on all the hot goss."

They got up with a huff and walked out of the conference room. Lustre was about to make their way after them when she was stopped by all three of their companions.

"Trust me, Commander," Kass said with big eyes. "They need some time."

"Time is the one-" She started.

"Thing we don't have," The ever-clever Kass finished her sentence for her. "Yes, Commander. And normally I'm down for those kinds of fatalistic cliches, but we have agents we need to organize, streets we need to clean, and mages to fight."

"But, the mage," She started again.

"Is irrelevant for now," Kass finished for her again. "Like they said, they have no idea what the Ardeleans are searching for, and they're not gonna tell us no matter what we do. So, let's put a compostable cap on the Romy issue for now and focus on what we *can* do. We can start with the vampires. The mages may be under this Covenant thing, but vamps are immune to that kinda shit, amirite Nico?"

Nico was shocked by her sudden take charge attitude, but quickly adapted. "Yes, Agent Al-Amin."

"Dude, we shared a shower for three years. You can quit it with the agent shit. Formalities and codes of conduct got thrown out the window the minute zombies started exploding."

"You do realize you're not in charge?" An entertained Lustre said as she leered down at the vibrant Sphinx.

"And yet I appear to be the only one acting like it."

Her eyes, as well as Nico's, widened. "Well… I dare say… behavior like that would normally result in a retired commission."

"And I will gladly accept said retired commission when I am not the most qualified field commander you have. I can track the vampires, keep them off my scent, bench press a couple hundred pounds, run twenty-five kilometers an hour - on a bad day - and can fly even faster than that. You need me, Sabrina."

Lustre was speechless. She cleared her throat and quickly pulled herself together. "Fine. Agent Al-Amin, I will leave field operations to you. I will continue coordinating with the other shelters and precincts, as well as try and get a hold of the local military's mystical response division."

"Yes, ma'am. And while you're at it, I need a tactical evaluation of all MIST operatives available at each precinct and shelter. I need to know if we still have loyal mages, and anybody experienced with Vampires. Werewolves, shapeshifters, pixies. Fuck, I'll take a Leprechaun if it means good luck. We need to get those blood suckin' bitches out of our city. Nico!"

He saluted out of habit. "Yes, ma'am!"

Kass giggled. "This is so much fun. You're on door duty. Nobody in or out without clearance."

"What kind of clearance?"

"The Alfie kind," She gestured to her extraterrestrial roommate.

"Yes, I can mentally scan those who enter for ill intent. I can also disable mages as I, too, am immune to their magic and can disrupt their Focuses."

"And that's why I love you, but you don't have to keep reminding us," Kass said with a sweet smile as she left the room to head back to the entrance doors. "I got the coordinates of every shelter and precinct answering our hails. I will make my way to each one, evaluate them, and report back as soon as I can. And if any kind of undead motherfucker gets in my way, they'll be even dead-er meat."

Nico, once again, felt compelled to hold her back. "Kass…"

"Nic. I know this may be weird and awkward, cuz we've told you this a thousand times, but you *need* to stay here. With Alfie. With Romy. With *Guy*. You are the most level-headed, resourceful, responsible, intelligent person any of us know. So, please, for me, for yourself, get your shit together and dust anybody who comes through that door that ain't waving the peace flag. Got it?"

He nodded. "Will do. Good luck."

"I'm off to find me a Leprechaun, motherfucker." The doors opened and, with a whip of her wings and a gust of wind, she flew out into the night once more.

Guy was mindlessly staring into the dark red abyss of the bay. He was neighbored by sleeping citizens and triage patients, some struggling more than others to keep their eyes closed. He was surrounded yet never felt more alone. Within him was a raging tempest of confusion and fear. Then he heard familiar footsteps behind him.

"Hi, Romy," he said, weakly.

Romy's reflection appeared in the window next to him. "Are you okay?"

"Of course, I am," he said, sarcastically. "Haven't you heard? I'm invincible."

"They didn't tell me everything. What all do you know?"

Guy held up a scalpel and stabbed himself in his own jugular.

"Heathen Gods!" Romy shouted as they covered their mouth for fear of sick coming out.

Blood gushed from his throat, but he somehow still had the power to pull the knife out, giving Romy a clear view of what was weighing so heavy on his mind. With a burst of scarlet energy, the blood returned to the opening in his neck as it healed itself in seconds. No scars. No blood. Nothing but a clean throat.

Romy's mouth was agape. They had seen healing spells before, but this was unprecedented in their experience.

"I have literally..."

"I know, right? Now, watch what happens when I do this."

Guy slashed his cheek, ever so gingerly. Unlike the wound he made earlier, it did not heal. It simply let out a small tribble of blood which Romy covered with their hand.

"It only heals fatal wounds," They deduced before activating their hue. "*Cura.*"

The cut healed.

"I can get hurt. I just can't die. Weird stuff, right?" He gave a hollow, sad chuckle.

"You don't have to tell me how not okay you are. And it is okay not to be okay..." They shook their head. "Fuck, I feel like such a turd for saying that. I can help. I know I can. Is there anything - *anything* - I can do for you?"

"It actually makes a lot of sense. I never actually got a chance to tell you how my parents died. It was my senior year. We were driving home from a band concert and arguing about what school I would go to. My parents – they were ridiculous – they wanted me to stay home, for Christ's sake. I wanted to see the world, pursue music... and then... out of nowhere."

Romy did not know what to say, so they just went with, "Oh, Guy…"

"I always wondered why I was the only one to survive the crash. They called it a miracle, proof that somebody's out there watching out for me." What once was a sunbeam smile had been eclipsed by a shadow covered frown. "Just tell me…" He started to choke up. "What am I? Where did… *this*… come from? Nico couldn't tell me, but I saw it in his eyes. I'm a *freak*."

Guy started to cry. Not knowing what else to do, Romy pulled him into a tight hug. "It's gonna be okay." Romy pulled back and looked at Guy's beautiful, somber face. They saw his tears and had a thought. "Hold onto this pain."

"What?"

"Just hold onto it," they said as they jumped to their feet and ran to the nearest medical tent.

They haphazardly ransacked it until they found what they were looking for: a beaker. Running back, they nearly knocked Guy over as they roughly placed the container beneath his crying eyes.

"Just hold still," they said while softly stroking his back. "I think I know exactly what to maybe do."

"Don't hold your breath for a vote of confidence," he said, as a tear dropped into the vial.

Romy smiled. "I won't."

"You're lucky you're cute."

"And you're lucky you're invulnerable. We all have our strengths, now let me use mine."

"What are you gonna do?"

Their response came in the form of a massive loogie hocked into the beaker.

"Blech!"

They looked at him sideways. "You just ripped a blood bank's worth of hemoglobin out of your neck, but snot makes you squeamish?"

"Excuse me for having upper limits."

They handed the beaker to Guy. "Hold this, please."

He took it, holding it ever so gingerly for fear of any of the contents spilling onto him. "What are you gonna do?"

They ripped off their boot and slammed it onto the ground, releasing the dirt and grime collected up in the crevices from the day's journey. They began to sort through the pile. They found a crest of dirt and sniffed it. "Graveyard soil." They scraped it off their finger into the beaker before picking up a strip of what looked like flesh. "Zombie meat."

Guy gagged. "Can we please hurry this up?"

"You can't hurry genius… or, at the very least, you shouldn't hurry somebody who's thinking on their feet." They tossed the dead flesh in with the rest of the ingredients and sloshed it around. "Now think lovely thoughts and pray that my Greek isn't as shitty as I think it is."

"What does that-"

"Shh!" They activated their Hue and began to glow a bright magenta which extended to the beaker. *"Hecate. Hecate. Epikaloúmai ti dýnamí sas. I dýnamí sou. I thélisí sas. Hecate. Hecate. Aftó to sóma brostá mou antistéketai sti diélefsi apó tin pórta. I pórta sou. Hecate. Hecate. Theá tis nýchtas. Theá tis zoís péra apó ti zoí. Sas parakaló. Apokalýpste ta mystiká mésa stin athánati psychí tou. Hecate."*

And with a flutter of magenta sparks, they tossed the battered brew in Guy's face. His eyes became magenta, to match Romy's as their two souls began to intermingle. Time slowed down around them. He fell back, but before he could hit the floor Romy caught him and placed their forehead on his.

Trying to access whatever magic was driving his immortality, Romy pushed their minds together only to see vivid images of Guy's childhood - smiling family, guitars, pianos, green fields. However, there was something lurking deep in the recesses of his heart. A knife piercing through him made of pure darkness. They reached out and touched it to gain some kind of deeper understanding, but this only sent them back to the waking world.

"What? What's wrong?" Guy asked, worried.

Romy was speechless. "I don't know... There's something inside you. Your mind. I might need to be a bit more invasive."

Guy's face became a gravestone. "Will it hurt?"

Romy grabbed his hand and stroked it gently. "Yeah... But it'll be fine. It'll still be me and I will work my damndest to make sure that you are comfortable and safe."

He sighed. "I trust you."

"I'm going to go into your mind. Now, aside from the pain, it's also going to be a very intimate experience. In order for me to freely explore your memories, I will have to give you my own."

"So, while you're strolling through my memory lane, I'll be getting pieces of you?"

"It's equivalent exchange. Not all magic comes for free."

"Is there anything you want me to know about before you start exposing yourself?" Guy tried making the tone seem light.

It nearly worked as he cast a sweet half-smile on Romy's face. "Please don't judge me."

"Hey," He pulled Romy's face up so they could see eye to eye. "I cannot put into words how much this means to me. You've saved my life and now you're willing to help me through this despite all that's going on. I know this might be the shared trauma talking, but I trust you… and if I could pick anybody on the planet to go rummaging through my memories, it would definitely be you."

Romy smiled and began to prepare the spell. Before they could get everything together, Guy gave them another inferno kiss. Allowing themself to get distracted, they leaned in, succumbing to his charms for a few moments before shaking back to reality.

"I need to focus." They looked at Guy sternly. "Lie down."

"Yes, master," he said playfully as he did what he was told. An instinct of his was to try to be fun and silly to off-set any serious issues going on around him.

Romy laid down next to him and held his hand. On the back of each of their wrists, they summoned a special glyph and took the plunge.

Romy was inside Guy's mind. A metaphysical labyrinth of doors. Romy entered the first one they could find.

"Actually, they're non-binary. Their pronouns are they-them, so they're not a boy."

If a disembodied astral form could blush, Romy's face would light up. Their knight in shining armor, ready to keep them from being misgendered by unknowing diner employees.

As part of the exchange, they gave up their own precious memory from that night.

"Well, fuck…" Romy accidentally said out loud as they watched Guy enter the diner.

The absurdly gorgeous man's absurdly gorgeous blue eyes scanned the room, met Romy's, and smiled a sunshine smile. Romy swooned and forgot Nico's name for a moment.

Romy stood up like they were meeting a prince. And for all they knew, he could have been one. *'Kiss me, and wake me up, you gorgeous man…'*

Another door.

"I think you and my roommate would get along," Alfie said as he showed Guy a cleverly cropped picture of Romy on his phone.

"Wow! They're gorgeous."

Another sacrificed memory.

They wanted to yell but could only muster a half-whisper. "Did I- did I do something?"

"No."

"Then why-" They fought back tears. They didn't cry. They hated crying. Crying in front of other people was something that only melodramatic attention seekers did. Romy did not want attention. They wanted to disappear. "Why?"

Another door. Guy getting accepted to work at the co-op counseling center.

Another sacrificed memory.

"You are hilariously dirty," A smiling Kass said, "and I want to be friends with you."

"I'll have to ask the spirits, but I think that can be arranged," they said with a wink.

Another door.

"Will it hurt?" A sixteen-year-old Guy asked his slightly older partner as they held each other on a blanket, under a night sky full of stars.

"Not as long as we keep kissing," the boy, Mark, said as he cradled him in his arms.

"Is it weird that I'm scared but also not scared at the same time?"

"It would be weird if you weren't. You know, we don't have to do this. We could just pack this up and I could take you back home."

Guy pondered. He thought, 'Maybe I should? But maybe I shouldn't? Do I want to lose my virginity to him? He's so amazing and so special but who's to say there won't be other equally amazing or special boys in my future?'

"Did you bring a condom?" Guy asked.

"Of course," Mark responded.

And Guy started kissing him again.

Another sacrificed memory. Romy's first time meeting another enby person.

"Being non-binary is like hearing everybody talk about how hot shit apples and oranges are when all you want is a peach or a pear or something outside the apple-orange binary. It's being too amazing for your essence and identity to be restricted to just one rigid idea of what gender looks like. Being enby means looking at those stupid pink and blue blankets they put us in when we were born and giving them the middle finger. We are more masculine than men and more feminine than women and fiercer than all the cis-het people in the world combined. Being enby means being a boss ass bitch, and I will never apologize."

They continued on. However, something pulled them away from their plotted course through Guy's mind. Something dark but benevolent.

They ran towards the sensation and opened the door farthest from where they entered. A door unlike all others. With a large infinity symbol over an inverted pentagram painted on it in what looked to be blood.

They opened the door and didn't find a memory. Only pure darkness. And a tall, statuesque woman draped in snakes and three faces protruding from all sides of her skull.

Hecate, Goddess of necromancy and the dark side of the moon.

Romy fell to their knees. "My queen. Is it truly you?

"Do you doubt your senses, fair mage?" *She asked in a soft, sugar sweet voice that echoed through all three mouths.* **"It is I. The queen of the night, Hecate."**

"My Goddess, why have you blessed me with your visage?"

You invoked me, young mage. I heard your cry, so I am here to help."

"Help in what way?"

This door protects a dark secret. So shrouded in pain, death, and torture that even I – a Great Goddess of the darkest magicks – would never allow one of my disciples to see it. But the answers you seek do not need to come from what is beyond this door. I will gladly and freely give it."

"My queen, to offer such a blessing without allowing me to give you a gift in return? I- I feel unworthy."

She held her hand out to stroke Romy's cheek. My dear necromancer, you will soon find out just how worthy you are. Your lover-"

"My Goddess, no offense but I don't wanna put labels on what me and Guy have. I mean – it's only been one date."

She stared at them with one eyebrow on each face raised, only slightly bemused. May I finish?"

Romy looked down at the astral ground. "Yes, madame."

Your love-" *She corrected herself.* "Guy – has been cursed by tainted magicks. He is neither capable of truly dying, nor truly living. He is un-living. A piece of his soul is bound to one who abuses my gift of necromancy to his own twisted ends and under a twisted God whose name even I refuse to let loose from my fabulous lips."

"So... he's..."

We dare not speak of it here. But go. Take this knowledge and use it to reclaim what has been taken from me."

Romy fell backwards onto the floor, the pure rush of meeting a Goddess enveloping them like a blanket of the smoothest silk. They were floored and energized. A sensation they could not put into words.

Guy felt similar. He felt warm and cold and hungry and full all at the same time. He quickly rushed to Romy's aid. "Hey! I'm here! Knight-in-shining-armor, gorgeous Guy, with my sunshine smile. Please tell me you're okay."

They quickly came to and remembered Hecate's words.

"You," they started, their voice faltering, still unable to process what their soul's eye had witnessed. "You're a Revenant."

Guy's mind quickly became lost as the sensation of having Romy within them fluttered away like a fleeting butterfly. "What... what's that?"

"You died once. But someone brought you back and now you can't die again. A Revenant is as close to a normal human that a zombie can get. You can age, you can get sick, you can get hurt, you just can't die."

"But… why me?"

The thousands of bells and alarms going off inside Romy's soul – a residual gift from Hecate's blessing – warned them of incoming danger. Activating their Hue, they summoned a powerful force field that protected against a great explosion. They stood tall while the others, sleeping quietly amongst the tents, flat beds, and sleeping bags were blown away like leaves. When the smoke cleared, Romy looked closer and became enraged at the most unwelcome sight imaginable.

"Hello, little brother," Daciana said with a wicked smirk, while being flanked by a cadre of a dozen Vampires. "It's been a long day for both of us, I'm sure, so why don't we just get straight to the point and you-"

A great wave of water slammed her into the nearby wall where it froze, trapping the cruel witch in its cold clutches.

Its source: Nicodemo Acquati.

"Hey, Daciana!" He said with a ferocious growl. "Get ready to have your butt handed back to you."

10

Bite the Dust

It was snowing in June. At first it started off as a light, cold breeze, only to evolve into a massive blizzard within a matter of hours. In what seemed like a split second, everything in the city was frozen over.

Thanks exclusively to Nico's command over water, he and Romy were the first to arrive at the State House after getting the call to action. This ability was also the reason he was recruited to join MIST's alpha task force during his very first cataclysm.

"Are you going to be okay here without me?" A worried, and partially co-dependent, Nico asked.

"Aww." Romy pouted their lips. "You're so cute. Of course, I'll be okay."

"It's just-"

"You're nervous. This is a big deal. This is your first alpha assignment! You should be proud of yourself, not worried about me."

"Yeah, but-"

"Sweetie," They put reassuring hands on his tight, nervous shoulders. "I'll be okay. You go. I'll stay. It'll give me some time to practice my card tricks. Okay?"

Nico smiled. "Okay. I love you."

"I believe you," Romy said, with a handsome half-smile. "I love you too.

They were about to kiss goodbye when they were interrupted by a great shout.

"Acquati!" Lieutenant Lustre called out.

"Yes, ma'am!" He responded with a salute. He turned to Romy. "I'll be back as soon as I can."

Romy waved as he marched away. They looked around at the large, empty room. The Beta MIST agents were guarding the doors while the mages were talking amongst themselves. Not sure what to do, they found an empty corner and sat quietly by themself. They pulled out their tarot deck and attempted to practice channeling spirits, hoping at least one might be open to a conversation about the weather.

After a few lonely moments, a sultry voice asked them a question. "Do you do readings?"

They looked up and saw the fiercest Sphinx they had ever met. She was also the second Sphinx they had ever met. Her MIST uniform was tailored perfectly to her tall and toned body. Her golden mane was organized into hundreds of ornate braids. Her pointed ears featured a dozen gold hoops between the two of them. Her sharp claw-nails were painted a shimmering gold. She looked as though she was worth a hundred karats.

Thus, they could not stop themself. "Wow! You are gorgeous!"

She blushed. "I know right. And thank you. You're quite the looker yourself."

"I very much appreciate that. I've been having a pretty sucky day, so any positive energy would be welcomed."

She raised a playful eyebrow. "Uh, have you seen the weather? Everybody's having a bad day."

"Valid."

"I'm Kass."

"Romy."

"Cute name. So, do you do readings?"

"I can, if you want, but I can't guarantee it'll be anything you like."

"Hey, I'd be happy with a simple 'low of fifty degrees.' Besides, I am bored."

They laughed. "Okay." They handed her the deck. "Shuffle it while counting to your favorite number."

It took her almost a full minute to finish. "There ya go."

They looked at her side-ways. "If I may be so bold, what number were you counting to?"

"Sixty-nine."

Romy contained a cackle. "Oh, so mature."

"It was almost four-twenty, but I thought that might take too much time."

Romy became excited. "Do you have pot?" They asked in a hushed tone.

She pretended to be shocked. "What?! Excuse you! Me?! A well-respected member of the very protectors of this here our beautiful city of - yeah, I'm packin'. But we're not allowed to cush on duty. Which is just making this very boring day even more boring."

"Tell me about it…"

"But maybe when the snow melts, you and I can toke it up in the alleyway?"

"I don't know, we'll have to see what's in the cards," they said, playfully. They spread the cards out in a line in front of her. "Pick three and set them out in front of you, left to right."

With an entertained smile, she did as she was told. "By the way, you're gay right?"

"Like a rainbow getting fisted."

She guffawed. "You are hilariously dirty, and I want to be friends with you."

"I'll have to ask the spirits, but I think that can be arranged," they said with a wink. They lifted the card to Kass's left. Nine of cups, reversed. "This card represents your past. Right side up, it means luxury, or financial fulfilment. But it's upside down. You came from great privilege, but it brought you no joy. In fact, you often felt like it was a burden."

Kass rolled her eyes. "That's a lovely punch on the nose."

They lifted the center card. "The hanged man. This represents your present. You managed to escape what you thought was a bad situation and are now working to provide for the world."

Kass gave a small smile. "Yeah, you know, just living that hashtag-best-life, hashtag-queen, hashtag-goals. Now, what does my future say?"

They lifted the rightmost card. "Death."

Kass's face dropped. "And here I thought everything was going so well."

"It's actually pretty okay. Death in tarot means metamorphosis. A fabulous change. Good or bad, either way it's going to lead to a new beginning."

"Huh. So, I guess, death is a good thing?"

They smiled. "It depends on your perspective."

Just then, the doors opened with a loud bang. Another MIST agent appeared. "Crisis averted. All mages, please prepare for debriefing, afterwards you can all go home."

"Debriefing?" Romy's eyebrow raised. "What does that mean?"

"It means they're gonna give you the four-one-one and then let you come smoke a joint with me while we discuss our life stories."

Romy smiled. "It's a date."

Kass flew high above the darkened city streets towards the JFK Library Shelter. Her feline eyes piercing through the black of the night, keeping watch for any possible threat. Unable to find one, she could not decide if she should be relieved or worried.

She pulled out her walkie-talkie. "This is Agent Al-Amin, to Shelter 4-B. Acting command please respond."

"Agent Al-Amin," A voice responded through heavy static. "This is Lieutenant Tomoe, we-"

Her ears twitched.

A rush of air.

A witch riding on a broomstick quickly flew into her line of sight. But it was not quick enough for her to evade Kass's fist. A sharp jab to her jaw sent her down to the ground below at an incredible velocity. For added measure, Kass snapped the broom in half and tossed the remains aside.

Hearing a heavy thud, she flew down to where the witch landed. Sure enough, she found the body of a dead-eyed, pale skinned, dark-haired young woman dressed in black and covered in tattoos identical to Romy's lying in a great pool of blood.

"Fuck…" This was the first time she had to kill in self-defense, and the fact that it was self-defense did not make it easier on her soul. She gave a heavy sigh. "Remember what the counselor said… 'Lethal force is never the solution, but self-defense is not murder. Lethal force is never the solution, but self-defense is not murder…'" She looked down at the corpse. "Hey sweetie… sorry for killin' ya. But, T-B-H, it's a little weird to see you all alone out here. As I recall, you were traveling with your coven, which means they're probz around her somewhere." She sniffed the witch to gain a semblance of the group's scent. "There were about ten of you, amirite? Guess, nine now… sorry, again, but I can tell you from personal experience that saying 'hi' with your fist is never the solution. Especially, when we both know…" A thought occurred to her. "We both know you wouldn't have stood a chance. You weren't trying to hit me, were you?"

"Not really," said a dark voice from above. Kass looked up to find eight mages, held aloft on their broomsticks. Raf, at the center, was standing on his like a surfboard. "But that's how life goes sometimes, isn't it? Accidents just happen."

"Sort of like how you were accidentally born with an ass for a face."

He clutched his chest in jest. "Oh, words can hurt, miss kitty."

"You think that hurts? Wait till you meet my claws."

"So confident, for a magic-less beast against the most powerful sorcerers on the planet."

"So confident, for someone who's using a large portion of his magical abilities to maintain the summoning ritual necessary to keep this town in terror." A subtle twitch in Raf's cheek showed Kass she had hit a nerve. She decided to put her degree in criminal psychology to good use. "Let me guess, you guys were trynna track me from up on high, hoping I might lead you to Romy, when miss thing down here's magic glitched out cuz you're all focusing your magic into keeping up this red cloud bullshit?" Every mage took on a dark, stoic facade. "That's what I thought. Question: with where you guys are at, power-level wise, do you honestly think you'd be able to fight someone who isn't standing half-mast? Or are the *most powerful sorcerers on the planet* as fragile as they look right now? Trembling on your flying dust collectors."

"Don't you have a litter box to fill?" Raf spat.

"Now, young man, I will not have you calling your mother names like that."

A series of "whoa's" overwhelmed the distracted spellcasters. Raf looked as if he were on the brink of boiling over.

"You wanna come up here and say that to my face?"

"Okay." And with a great flap of her wings, she was in his face. "Your mom's my litter box, you sad bag o'dicks."

He tried to give her a solid right hook, but she blocked it with her left arm. And, with one solid punch to his face, sent him flying off his broom.

"Raf!" One of the witches called out as she flew down to catch him.

The others insidiously surrounded Kass, giving her the opportunity to do a headcount.

"Six of you versus lil' ol' me? How unfair… for you."

A warlock on her flank began to cast. *"Aprindere!"*

But Kass heard his throat and hand move before the spell exited his mouth. As a great fireball launched from his palm, she flew upwards, sending a gust of wind that blew the flames back at the caster.

Making a sharp nosedive downwards, she goaded the mages with a sassy "Meow!"

She zigged and zagged through the air, around street-lamps, telephone poles, through tight alleyways, before folding her wings back in and landing on the ground with a suave tuck and roll.

Looking up, Kass watched as all the mages above haphazardly waved their glowing hands, preparing assault spells. Their lack of focus was making it difficult for them to finish the casting. Capitalizing on their impotence, Kass pulled the door off a nearby abandoned car and threw it up at them, interrupting their casting and causing them to scatter like flies.

A subtle quickening in the air as her hair stood on end and everything became hot.

Kass flipped back to dodge a bolt of magical lightning thrown at her by the now grounded Raf, wearing an emerald Hue. Watching him prepare a second charge, she noticed a utility access hole cover beneath her and pulled it up, using it as a shield as the aggro mage threw his spell. As he recharged, she tossed the plate at him. However, just before it was about to hit his head, it was halted by a magical force field cast by a nearby witch.

"You guys don't go down easy, do you?"

The witch responded with a sick smile. She started to vomit, causing the Sphinx to repel in disgust.

"Oh, my Gods, ew-ew-ew-ew-ew-ew-ew! Is she possessed?! Does she need a doctor?! What the fuck, girl???"

Looking up at Kass with sad eyes, she activated her orange Hue and enveloped the bile with it. The spew began to grow and mold itself until it became a great, gargantuan, human-shaped golem.

"Oh, fuck that!" Kass said. "I'm fighting barf monsters now?"

Her wings popped out of her back, and she flew backwards into the sky. A witch attempted to catch her off guard by flying into her, only to be caught off guard herself by Kass's foot to her jaw. She grabbed the witch's broomstick, spanked her into the ground with it, before snapping it in half and tossing it to the ground.

The barf monster started throwing debris up at Kass. Her swift reflexes kept her safe, but she was keenly aware the beast was trying to distract her so the mages floating above could prepare their battle magic. As a bench was tossed up at her, she grappled it with her hands and feet and redirected it up at the mages. As she expected, they scattered, and when it came back down, she seized it once more and tossed it at the witch summoning the monster.

With the sorceress distracted, the monster became too disoriented, giving Kass a window of opportunity to swiftly swoop down and deliver a wonderfully solid punch to the woman's face. The force of the strike sent her flying back into the wall behind her. With her knocked out, the vomit monster returned to its liquid form, spreading out over the ground near Kass's feet.

"EW-EW-EWWWWWW!" She screamed as she flew upwards. "How does she live with herself, knowing that's a thing she can do?"

Raf approached. "You think our magic is gross, beast? How quaint…" He gestured to yet another dark-haired sorcerer floating above him. "Lazar? Why don't you show the fleabag how gross our magic can be?"

He descended and chuckled in his throat as his mahogany Hue activated. Kass started to hear the sound of hundreds of insect wings fluttering around her. The mage was manipulating the insects in the area into a great, choreographed ribbon that flew at her.

She tried to fly up, but another mage lassoed her foot with what appeared to be glowing, red, liquid rope. With one whiff, she quickly figured out what it was.

"Is that your blood, you human kidney stone?!"

She took a closer look and saw that the magicked blood was seeping from a great wound on his palm. The bugs started to swarm around her and began picking at her hair and her flesh. It was a light torture she knew she could endure, but not for long.

Suddenly, the bugs stopped, and the blood rope melted away. And a friendly voice filled her ears.

"I apologize for any delay in my assistance," Alfie said as he emerged from the shadows. "I do not possess the speed required to have made a timelier entrance into the fray."

She looked down and saw the mages all frozen in place. Alfie's psychic hold on them kept them not only from using their magic but from moving as well.

"Alfie?" She descended to his level and wrapped her wings up into her body. "Not that I'm not glad to see you, but shouldn't you be at the shelter?"

"That is the reason I am here. You need to come back with me."

"Why?"

"The shelter is under attack. Daciana, sister to Romy, is leading the charge with a cadre of vampires, and Raf, the mage you were fighting only moments ago, has turned invisible and I can no longer sense him."

"What?!" She quickly turned to look only to receive an invisible kick to her stomach.

Her muscular resistance, though tested, enabled her to rebound from this strike, grab the unseeable leg, and toss its owner up against the nearby wall. Out of thin air, Raf reappeared, having undergone a wicked transformation.

His skin had become green, like Alfie's, and a singular antenna was poking out of his forehead. Yet his ears had become pointed, almost feline, and his teeth turned into fangs. One eye shimmered a bright yellow as his other took on a pale pink. All while his entire body was glowing a bright emerald Hue.

He bounced off the wall and up onto a streetlamp with a graceful agility that rivaled Kass's.

"Impressed?" He said with a cocky sneer. "It's a fun little talent I call 'MirrorMirror.' It's sort of an 'anything you can do, I can do better,' magic."

The other mages, having recovered from Alfie's empathic enchantment, reawakened, and seemed prepared to continue the fight.

"No, guys," Raf instructed. "Head back to HQ. Leave these creatures to me."

They nodded and activated their Hues. Reaching out with their magic, they summoned their broomsticks to their hands. And off they flew, sparing only a moment to pick up the sorceresses Kass had knocked out moments ago.

Kass used her peripheral vision to get a brief glance at Alfie. He was hiding his fear with a great amount of fortitude. He was not the warrior Kass was. She needed to get him out of there.

"How about we make a deal, mage? I let you go, and you let me go. We both have wounded we need to see to, and I think that supersedes this kind of scuffle."

"Hmmm," He pretended to consider it. "No. I refuse to drop the opportunity to put a bitch in her place."

With a rough grunt, a pair of hideous, fleshy wings burst out of his back, ripping through his shirt. They began rapidly molting feathers. The sight was nearly enough to make Kass nauseous.

"This night has really been testing the limits of my stomach."

With another grunt, Raf flew at her. With swift cunning, she flew up to dodge him, but with equally swift cunning, he grabbed at her leg and tossed her into Alfie, knocking his head into the wall behind him.

For the first time in a long time, Kass was winded, but pushed herself to check on her friend. "Alfie? Sweetie?" He was alive, but unconscious.

Raf descended to the ground next to her, and callously leered. "You know, you're kinda cute when you're all feeble like this. If I weren't worried about catching ringworm, I'd ask you out."

Both Raf and Kass's ears twitched.

He looked out into the distance to see a great inferno. It's source: the Seaport Shelter.

Taking advantage of his distraction, she did a sweeping kick and floored him before pulling Alfie into her arms. Without looking back, she flew up into the sky towards the blast.

She flew as fast as she could.

But it was not fast enough.

She saw a towering blaze blocking the entrance to the shelter. She saw Romy, standing before the inferno, with a strange staff in their hand, Guy at their side, and Daciana lying in defeat before them.

"Romy!" She called out.

But they were deaf to her calls.

A flash of red lightning blinded her, forcing her into an emergency landing onto the roof of a nearby drug store.

She looked up. The fire remained, but everybody had disappeared.

"What the fuck?" She whispered, in total awe.

A great flood of water from within the shelter extinguished the flames. Nico appeared, dragging a pale-skinned youth by the collar of his shirt.

"Nico!"

He looked up at her. "Kass, where's Romy?!"

"Kass?" Alfie said, as he stirred beneath her.

"Alfie? Are you okay?" She got up and lifted him to his feet.

"Yes. I sensed Romy, but then they became gone."

"Yeah, they just vanished. Where do you think they went?"

"I do not know. I am unable to sense them." Alfie looked down at Nico and identified the boy he was strongarming. "Ianto…"

"Ianto? Like, as in your brother?"

He jumped into her arms. "Quickly, we must join them."

Kass did as she was told and swiftly flew the two of them down to meet Nico and his vampiric prisoner, bound in chains made of ice.

"Serious fear, worry, confusion, and depression, yet incredible hints of excitement and violence-fueled adrenaline." Alfie said in a straight monotone voice.

"Hello, Alfie…"

"What happened?" Kass asked.

Nico just stared at her with dead eyes as he tossed Ianto to the ground. "A lot…"

11

Undead or Alive

A sunny day in Cambridge, Massachusetts. A small cafe along Main Street. Two nineteen-year-olds enjoying hot cups of herbal tea.

Romy and Nico.

The two were in all the same casting seminars together, thus they were in all of the same study groups and went to all of the same parties where they would sit in the corner, too nervous to join the rest of the crowd, and too invested in whatever conversation they would be having together.

Every time their eyes met, it felt like fireworks. They were stupid in love. Unfortunately, both were truly too awkward to do anything about it.

Romy was still in the midst of their own gender dilemma. Meeting other gender non-conforming, non-binary people had sent their cis-presenting self into a tailspin. All while dealing with the culture shock, coming from a coven, while juggling an immense scholastic workload. They went from being isolated from the rest of the world, to being surrounded by a diverse collection of people at one of the most prestigious universities in North America. A university where they found friendship and support for the first time in their life.

Meanwhile, Nico was trapped in an uncomfortable body binder. He was on hormones that were causing him to gain weight in the most unwanted places. He had mood swings that made it hard for him to maintain his Focus. And to top it all off, it made him uncomfortably horny nearly all the time. It took the hottest chamomile tea to keep him from humping Romy's leg at that very moment.

Romy may have been too squeamish to admit their feelings for him, but they were able to tell when Nico needed a moment away from studying. Thus, a tea break.

With the conversation dwindling, and wanting to impress him, Romy decided to try something brave. "Hey, wanna see a trick?"

He smiled. "What kind of trick?"

Romy pulled out a deck of playing cards.

"Oh no!" He started to laugh. "Please tell me you do not do stage magic."

Romy worked hard to contain a cackle. It had become a habit after months of glares and weird looks. Cackling was a big Ardelean trait that they used to be proud of, until they began to realize being an Ardelean was not necessarily a good thing.

"'*Stage magic*' is a terrific way to test out glamours, allocation spells, and it's also just cutesy fun. Making everybody ask 'is it really magic? Are they a mage or just a phony? *Why would you put a bird there?!*'"

"Is that why you wear handcuffs as a bracelet? Or is that a kinky thing?"

Romy looked down at their wrist. The souvenir of their very first magic trick shackled around it. "Yeah. I love magic. And I especially love magic that makes people happy."

"Aren't you a necro-major?" Nico said to make Romy think he wasn't as icy as his peers thought he was.

"And you're studying to be a healer, but I *know* you want to be a battle mage."

Nico smiled. "So, do you have a trick for me? Or what?"

Romy quickly shuffled the cards, then handed the cards to Nico. "Shuffle."

Nico scoffed but did as he was told before handing them back. "Now what? You gonna make me pick a card?"

"Well, if you're just gon' spoil everythin', then I don't see the point in this."

He blew a playful raspberry at them and pulled the card from the top of the deck.

Ace of hearts.

A slight flutter.

"Now put it back."

A sweet sigh as he replaced the card. He watched as Romy shuffled and shuffled before placing the deck back on the table. Then, they activated their Hue, which gleamed a beautiful, magenta light over the cards. They began to float and fly about in such beautiful acrobatic choreography that Nico, who had been raised around flamboyantly extravagant mages, could not help but gape.

After a minute of this flashy display, Romy grabbed a card in mid-air and proudly presented it to Nico. "Is this your card?"

Ten of clubs.

He laughed through his nose. "Good golly, Miss Molly. Stop. After all that show-offy magic, you pick the wrong card?"

Romy looked baffled. "This isn't your card?"

Despite feeling sorry for them, he could not stop smiling. "No. It is not. But it was still a cool spell."

"Huh… well," He looked past Nico out the window. "What about that one?"

"What?" He said, confused.

He turned around and saw a large moving truck parked outside the cafe. "Home is where the heart is! Put an ace up your sleeve!" was painted in massive letters on its side. Along with its logo: a door-sized Ace of Hearts card.

Nico turned back to Romy with wide eyes. "How did you do that?"

They smiled. "A good magician never reveals their secrets."

Romy did not know it at the time, but that was the very moment they stole Nico's heart.

Daciana stared at Nico with dead, angry eyes, still trapped between the wall and the sheet of ice he had pinned onto her. He stared right back, unafraid, and unyielding.

"I know you…" She said as her eyes glowed a violent violet and fire erupted from inside her, melting the ice trap. "You're the Legacy my brother abandoned the Coven for. You're…" She looked him up and down with a sneer. "… smaller than I thought you'd be."

He did not respond with words. Instead, he pressurized the sewer pipes lining the shelter, pulling water out from the roof, floor, and wall. With his mind, he summoned great blades of ice, levitating them in the air around his head. Normally, this intimidated his foes, but she was less than impressed.

"Ooh, fancy. I guess I can kinda see why he'd-"

A rush of magenta infused debris hit her from her blindside, knocking her to the ground. Her vampire underlings pointed their guns at the source.

"Daciana!" Romy called out. "Stand down or I'll put you down."

She quickly got back up onto her feet. "Ugh… well, now here I was thinking I'd be able to slay your little water slinging boyfriend before moving onto the-"

Romy threw another Hue-infused mound of debris at her before giving Nico a knowing look. Their minds in sync, he activated his ice blue Hue and produced a sigil made of pure ice in the air before infusing it with his magic. On the other side of the room, Romy summoned an identical sigil made of magenta light.

In complete unison, they cast their spell. *"Desterrar!"*

Romy's magenta magic and Nico's ice blue magic fused to immerse the room in a lavender light, removing every MIST agent and refugee from the room, teleporting them to another shelter. That brand of spell could only be performed in perfect tandem by multiple casters. Summoning this power left Nico and Romy exhausted. But not spent.

Daciana's face was void of any emotion save annoyance. "Well, there go my hostages…"

"There is still one, madame," a vampire Romy identified as Ianto, Alfie's brother, said as he pointed out Guy, hiding behind Romy.

"Well, then," Daciana covered herself in violet flames only for them to be immediately snuffed. "What?"

"What is happening?" Ianto asked.

Alfie appeared in the doorway. "Aggression centered around high amounts of anxiety, fear, greed, insecurity, envy, and ego. You have a very complicated mind. If you were capable of rehabilitation, I would offer my services as a mental health counselor."

"Alfie's an empath, Daciana," Romy announced. "He can block your Focus. So, how about you and your suck-buddies surrender while you still can?"

Ianto pointed his pistol at his brother. "Alfie."

He kept his cool under the pressure. "Ianto."

The vampire was about to fire when Nico summoned a whip of water and slapped the gun out of his hands. "Alfie, get out of here!"

The other vampires held their guns and pointed them indiscriminately at each of them.

Alfie stood firm, focusing his attention on Daciana. "No."

"Alfie, it's okay," Romy said. "Find Kass. Find *anybody*. Get help. We can take care of this.

Alfie could not deny Romy's confidence in the face of mortal danger. Releasing his hold on Daciana, he quickly ran for the exit. The vampires opened fire on him only to be blocked by a thick wall of ice.

"Surrender now or face dire consequences," Nico commanded, his gentle voice taking on great power and strength.

Daciana responded by summoning her violet flames once again. "It's been a very long day and I'm not here for you, so just die."

She threw a fireball at Nico, which he deflected with a splash of water before sending his ice blades flying at her. She threw bolts of fire to block them. Her Hue made her look as if she were about to explode when a rush of magenta light flew at her, dragging her out of the shelter. Nico looked where Romy and Guy once stood together, but only the immortal golden boy remained.

He turned his attention back to the vampires. "Get out now, or else."

"Funny," Ianto said as he picked his pistol up. "I was about to say the same thing to you."

"What do you even want?"

Ianto pointed his gun at Guy. "Him."

Guy's face became white as snow. "Me?"

Nico quickly figured it was connected to his strange healing powers. "That's not an option."

"Well, it must be an option or else we are going to kill *you*."

Nico rolled his eyes before summoning a massive wave that swept up the vampires. He manipulated the torrents within to rip the guns out of their hands, taking them apart piece by piece, before slamming them against the wall and trapping everything but their heads in a thick sheet of ice.

"Shit," was all Ianto could say as he realized how screwed they were.

"I have questions and I expect them to be answered," Nico said with a stare as cold as the ice floating about.

"Or what?" One of the other vampires spat at him.

Nico responded by summoning a tentacle of water that flew into the talkative vampire's mouth and froze around his fangs, digging deep into his gums before ripping them out of his skull. He screamed with his whole body as his black vampire blood spilled out onto the frozen wall.

"AAAAAAAAARRGGGGHHH!"

The bloody fangs, encased in ice, levitated before Ianto's eyes.

"Your name is Ianto, correct?"

"What of it?" he said, desperately trying to hide his fear.

"Tell me who you work for."

"Daciana, is that not obvious?"

"She's not smart - or sane - enough to orchestrate something like this. Someone recruited her and that same person recruited you. Who was it?"

Ianto rolled his eyes, aware of the futility of resistance. "Somebody by the name of Henry Tooth."

"Henry Tooth?"

"Yes, we were officially hired by Daciana, but she was acting under orders of a man named Henry Tooth."

"Who is he?"

"I only know him through the paper trail, we have never met in person. When Daciana approached us, offering us as much money as she did to do the things she wanted us to do, I knew an investigation would be necessary. Only a fool signs a deal with the devil without checking the fine print. And I wanted to know who the bigger devil was, Daciana or myself."

"And you realized that the real devil was Henry Tooth…" Nico ruminated on this.

Guy approached the frozen wall of vampires. "What does he want with me?"

"I do not know, nor do I care."

"They just hired you to kidnap him without telling you why?" Nico pointedly asked.

"Of course. Realistically speaking, if you were planning mass murder, would you truly want a bunch of mercenary vampires knowing the intricate details? Given the circumstances, he made the right call. You have successfully captured us, and we have no way of providing you the information you seek."

Nico groaned in frustration. "What do you know, then?"

"I know where their lair is. I know how to get in. And I know that, right about now, Daciana is working tirelessly to wear your Romy down until they give her what she wants."

"And what is that?" Nico asked.

"The Demiurge."

"The Demiurge?" Guy's face scrunched as he turned to Nico. "What's that?"

"I have no idea," Nico said and turned back to Ianto. "What do you know about it?"

"The name and nothing else."

"How do I know you're not lying?"

"You cannot. You can only divine that I have no intention of losing my teeth."

An explosion came from outside that dragged the attention of all except the vampires. They capitalized on the moment by transforming into bats, escaping their icy confines and flying out into the night. Ianto was about to join them, but Nico summoned a blade of ice and pressed it into his neck.

"BASTARDS!" He yelled out at them. "GET BACK HERE!" But his demand fell on pointy deaf ears. Forced to closely examine his situation, he realized he had no other options. "So… I guess we are going to have to work together now, are we not?"

"We are *not* going to be working together," Nico said with the straightest face. "You are going to take me to Tooth's hideout. You are going to help us defeat and capture him, after which you will surrender to Boston MIST's authority - *peacefully* - and I will make sure that the sentencing committee recognizes your compliance."

Ianto raised a heavy eyebrow at him and then looked over at Guy who gave him a shrug. "Which is worse: prison or death?"

"I am thinking…" He ponders for a moment and sighs with an eye roll. "Fine. I accept the terms of my surrender."

"Good," Nico said as he melted the ice encasing Ianto and summoned a great wave that carried them out into the city streets while simultaneously shackling the vampire.

"Oh, wonderful… Now I am wet *and* shackled. This is turning into the night of my life…"

They were immediately met by a wall of fire. Just as Nico was about to extinguish it, Guy called out.

"Romy?!"

Nico looked up and squinted through the intensity of the blaze. Sure enough, Romy was standing over Daciana a few yards away. The two had been through an intense battle as the very foundation of the ground around them looked like it had been struck by a meteor. Romy was holding a strange staff that Nico could barely make out.

Seeing that they had not answered Guy's call, Nico echoed loudly. "ROMY!"

But they did not answer.

Without thinking, Guy leapt through the fire.

"What are you doing?!" Nico yelled at him, to no avail.

Guy ran at Romy. Out of nowhere, a great flash of red light blinded Nico and Ianto. When they turned their gaze back onto the scene, Daciana, Romy, and Guy were all gone without a trace.

"No!" Was all Nico could say as he summoned a wave of water to put out the flames before them.

Just then, he heard Kass's voice from above. "Nico!"

He looked up and found her sitting atop a building with Alfie at her side. "Kass, where's Romy?!"

"Ugh," Ianto groaned as he watched his brother and Kass descend before them.

Alfie noted Nico's demeanor and could not help but channel his ever-amplifying internal issues. "Serious fear, worry, confusion, and depression, yet incredible hints of excitement and violence-fueled adrenaline."

"Hello, Alfie…"

"What happened?" Kass asked.

Nico just stared at her with dead eyes as he tossed Ianto to the ground. "A lot…"

Example of a Mage's ID:

ML#: N-787292   ISS: 07/02/2019   MAGICAL LICENSE
                 EXP: 04/17/2024

HEDGE, Romy

DISC: Necromancy

SEX: Non-Binary

DOB: 04/17/1992

WGT: 140 lbs.   HGT: 5'10"   HAIR: Brown   EYES: Brown

Photocopy: Not for use as actual identification

DISCIPLINE: Necromancer

UNSPOKEN WORD: "SoulSpark"

Capable of utilizing energized hue to produce

hard light constructs or telekinetically possess

solid matter, often focused via hands.

12

HellFire

An "Unspoken Word" was the traditional term that refers to the magical phenomena a mage could summon without the use of an incantation or sigil. "A word-less spell. The unspoken word." Most, if not all, modern mages refer to these skills as "powers." For the purpose of maintaining order, as many powers were quite similar, mages were encouraged to give their powers names. And then, with time, the name became a necessity for getting a license to practice magic. Romy always called theirs "SoulSpark," but almost chose "FingerBlast," as a joke. Nico vetoed this without a second thought.

"You can't be serious..."

"I'm not trying to be," they said with a mischievous grin.

"Romy, it's going on your official license!"

"FingerBlast!" They said while making finger guns and laser noises. "I could shout it out every time I use my powers! Like Sailor Moon!"

"Gods, no!"

"I'm kidding! I'm kidding!" They actually weren't, but they didn't want Nico to hate them forever. They found the whole concept to be a joke, so they could never properly take it seriously.

After their powers manifested during that fateful confrontation with Daciana, it didn't take long for them to start finessing their telekinetic motor control. A finesse which developed through subtle acts of rebellion against the oppressive regime of their "Aunt" Bogdana and Daciana.

Whenever Daciana would knock over a beloved crow's nest or "accidentally" burn their Bună's garden, she would soon after find herself mysteriously pelted with twigs and pebbles. Bună, with knowing eyes, was quick to blame it on the birds. At fifteen, in a fury, she retaliated and set a tree ablaze, which nearly caused a forest fire. For the first time in Romy's life, they got to witness their older sister get punished.

Bogdana, as the more difficult target, was where Romy developed their laser-point precision. She was one of three coven mages in charge of the children's schooling and would often pack her days with chastising Romy over the smallest slights.

"Your sigils are wonky. You're not conjugating your Romanian properly. If I were a Goddess, I'd sooner smite you than bless you with my power." She would often decorate these criticisms with colorful language. "Girly-boy. Pansy. Curist."

Every time she did, Romy would move her desk to the left, one centimeter at a time. They would drop pieces of ceiling into her tea. During one daring day, they moved her glasses from where she left them on the table to the top of her head. Yet since Bogdana was so convinced of Romy's lack of power, she never thought that they were behind all the mischief. She had become certain the schoolhouse was haunted. She scheduled an exorcism.

'What kind of necromancer can't tell the difference between telekinetic harassment and a poltergeist,' Romy thought to themself.

When Daciana went to Bucharest to attend the Romanian Institute of Necromancy, Romy began to truly come into their own. At that point, their Bună had taken on the sole responsibility of training them. It was through her that they learned to summon sigils from memory, to bend the light of their Hue into shapes as simple as circles and as complex as three-dimensional butterflies. They learned that pranks and screwing with their garbage family members wasn't their only talent.

"You can do anything, my dear," She would say to them, anytime they allowed Bogdana or Daciana's cruel words to get to them. "It matters not what fools think of you. Only what you think of yourself. And as long as you *know* you are great, you will be *greater*."

It was these words that echoed through Romy's mind as they used their powers to bulrush Daciana where she stood at the entrance of the mired shelter. Just before she was about to smite their ex-lover.

"It's been a very long day and I'm not here for you, so just die."

She threw a fireball at Nico. All the fury rushing through Romy's heart put them in a tailspin. They activated their Hue and flew at her, grabbing her and dragging her out of the shelter. Once outside, they dropped her onto the ground like trash before finishing their dash a few yards away.

"Well…" She said, her face covered in dirt and fury. "That was cute."

They levitated several bits of shrapnel lying on the ground and threw them at her.

She summoned a shield made of pure heat to protect herself.

"Rude!" She said, as if scolding a child.

Romy had had enough with her attitude. "What the fuck is wrong with you? You have destroyed countless lives and you're standing there, making jokes? Like nothing is wrong?"

She scoffed and looked at them like a clown in a carnival. "Oh no, a bunch of *plebeians* died. How awfully terrible and terribly awful. Punish me! Lock me in a prison and throw away the key!" She cackled so forcibly, as if she wanted to sound like a monster.

Romy responded by throwing a car at her.

Before it could make an impact, Daciana summoned flames beneath her feet, launching her into the air. Conjuring a glyph mid-flight, she used it as a pedestal to regain her footing.

"Such teeth…" She said.

"Wait until you see my claws." They cast their spell, "*Varteja*," and summoned a massive whirlwind that threatened to throw her from her perch.

She tilted backwards and used the symbol as a shield against the great gust before throwing a great ball of fire at Romy's face.

They countered by quickly forming a protective bubble around themself.

While standing on her floating platform, she produced a volley of spitfire flames that hit the shield like machine gun bullets.

Despite the harsh assault, their confidence - the strength behind their magic – continued unyielding.

They used their magic to conjure a rope and, with their keen eye and wrist, lassoed Daciana's leg. With a great tug, she was yanked off her metaphysical pedestal.

Refusing to fall, she held onto her glyph with all her strength while summoning a barrage of flames.

She missed by a few yards. Knowing that she was a better shot, Romy looked towards where the fire landed and saw an overturned car with gas trickling out the side.

A great explosion ignited the night. Both were able to protect themselves against the blast, in great thanks to the third eye tattoos enhancing their intuition. They went tumbling to the ground.

Romy had to stop to catch their breath and allow their blinded eyes to adjust. Daciana had no interest in waiting.

"Prinde." She wrapped Romy up in a magical body cage and lifted them high into the air. "Cute effort, sweetie. But did you forget that *I'm* the battle mage here?"

"If I forgot anything it's how easy it is to lose against a lunatic. *Eliberarea.*" Their Hue ignited and obliterated the mystic prison.

Mimicking Daciana's earlier spell, they summoned a pedestal glyph, but reinforced it with another that cast a series of lightning bolts at Daciana's feet.

Being the expert fighter that she was, she dodged every one of the strikes. In an effortless dance, she released small flames out from under her feet. casting several sigils into the street with scorch marks. Imbuing them with her Hue, the earth rose and gathered into a great granite spear.

Daciana. *"Azvârli!"*

It flew at Romy like a torpedo.

Romy. *"Sfărâma!"*

The lance exploded into several great fragments that were deflected back at Daciana.

She threw up a shield glyph but, instead of hitting her with the shards, Romy pierced the ground around her in a star formation.

Romy. *"Detuna!"*

The spears ignited.

Daciana. *"Puterea mea. Verso."*

The flames became wrapped up in her violet Hue. She threw the collected inferno up at her sibling. They only barely dodged the assault by leaping onto a nearby lamp post.

"Echilibru." Their balancing spell kept them from falling off the steep perch.

Daciana was out of breath. "How… are you… so good at this???" she said under her breath.

Unfortunately for her, Romy's ears were as keen as their fighting skills. "How are you so bad at this?"

"You really should... give up... you know…"

"Really? And why's that?"

"Cuz you… you know… I'll win…"

"I think you know that neither one of us believes that." They shot her a look usually reserved for bugs. As if they were watching her struggle to escape a fly trap.

Their intent was to irritate, and she was irritated. "If you surrender, I promise no harm will come to anybody else."

"Oh, we're makin' promises now, are we? You must really be desperate." They smiled a wicked smile.

She tossed a fireball.

They conjured another SoulSpark lasso. They flung it at a nearby lamp post. With less grace than they had hoped, they descended to the ground with a light tumble.

She tried to take advantage of this clumsy moment with another blast of flame only for them to quickly counter with a reflective shield that sent the blast flying back at her, forcing her to cower behind a demolished car.

"While we're chatting, *sis*… why don't you fill me in on what it is I'm s'posed to hand over to you."

Her response came in the form of several enchanted power lines, lashing at them like tentacles.

Romy's telekinetic capabilities, however, were far more formidable. The wires turned to their command with but a flick of their wrist. Turning them on her, they flew at the car Daciana was hiding behind. With great ease it was lifted off the ground, exposing her.

"Not feelin' chatty anymore, gurl? I thought you were the queen of battle magic! Or am I confusing 'battle magic' with 'fruitlessly gloating and putting people down as a means of controlling them in order to pre-empt fights that you know you can't win'?"

"AAARGH!" With a roar and a blast of flame, she threw the car out of its wiry confines and into Romy's direction.

Conjuring a magical buzzsaw, they sliced through it.

Daciana leapt at them like a velociraptor, emerging between the split halves with burning hands ready to scorch Romy's face.

Summoning a massive, magical fly swatter, they smacked her into the ground like a mosquito.

"You really don't get it, do you, *older sister*?"

She looked at them with venomous eyes. Yet, no venomous remarks left her lips as she got back onto her feet.

They continued. "You know, I used to think your Focus was anger. Or hate. Then I thought you got your powers from selfishness or greed. Then, for a couple years, I thought it could possibly be envy."

She spat on the ground before throwing another fireball.

Without flinching, they blocked it and sent a bolt of psychic lightning flying at her.

Despite being run ragged, she still managed to dodge and weave like a frightened yet agile rat.

They went on. "For a teeny, tiny portion of my life, I used to think that all the times you hit me or burned me or cast hexes on me were out of *jealousy*!"

She cackled and skeptically put down their words. "Jealous? Me? Of *you*!"

"I know! It sounds ridiculous. And it took me forever. Fuck, I prob'ly wouldn'a figured it out without Alfie's help, if I'm honest."

"And what's that, my little *curist*."

They were many yards away from each other, but Romy may as well have stared her dead in the eyes point blank. "*Fear.*"

A twitch in her right eyebrow betrayed her truth. And precipitated another scorching heat wave that Romy, again, deflected.

Then, delicious words formed at the back of their mouth, flying outward with an angelic melody Romy could never describe. "You're afraid of me."

"Don't make me laugh!" She yelled.

Another fireball. Another dodge.

Another bolt of lightning. Another leap.

"Daciana, c'mon! It's so obvious how scared you are. When I was born, you were afraid that our parents would love you less - cuz you're a walking entitled older sister stereotype. So, you treated me like shit. Then you got scared that I would eventually get strong enough to stand up to you. So, you started burning me. Then you got scared that I'd threaten your rise to power in the coven. So, you tried to break my spirit. And now, now after all that you've done, you're here, face to face with the one person you've spent your entire life trying to destroy, and you're afraid… cuz you know you're gonna lose."

"Shut up!"

Another fireball.

Another bolt of lightning.

"Here's the rub though: my Focus is Confidence. And if there's anything I've never been more confident about, it's that I can kick your ass."

They were just a couple of months shy of graduating college when the news broke. Doina Ardelean, High Mage of Romy's coven, their mentor, and their Bună, had died peacefully in her sleep.

Their father, Maron, was now the High Mage. And Daciana, who had acquired an incredibly large following after becoming "witch famous," was next in line. This fame doubled the Ardelean Coven's membership. And tripled the size of her toxic ego.

And while Romy was studying to become a necromancer and rejoin their coven, they had fallen in love. A love
they shared with a Legacy – a mage raised in a wealthy magical
family outside of the covens. A love that they knew their family
would never accept. And with Bună dead, they could not find
a good reason to go back. And being a hedge mage would be
worth it if it meant being with Nico for the rest of their life.

And so, they drove. The drive was fifteen hours that
they split up over two days, with a stop in a small park to sleep
in the backseat. They did not want to leave the car. They were
too afraid that if they did, they would run away.

It was a sunny, muggy Georgia morning. The Ardelean
Coven grounds were thirty minutes outside Savannah city limits in the Deep Woods. The entrance was guarded by a great
gateway marked with their family motto: "Cast Spells. Never
Doubts."

"Never doubts…" They said to themself with a heavy
heart thumping away in their chest. Taking a deep breath, they
activated their Hue and cast the spell to open the gates. "*Ar-
delea - sunt acasa.*"

The mouth of their own personal hell opened, and they
drove down the gravel road.

There were children outside, practicing spells, playing,
or feeding the ravens. As soon as the young Ardeleans saw
their car, they ran inside to tell their parents of Romy's arrival.

The road led them straight to their childhood home, the largest house in the settlement and the only one standing above a single floor. The exterior looked like nothing more than a simple, cheap, aged shack of a house, but its inside was enchanted to look like a gorgeous Georgia mansion, a reflection of their Florida-born mother's indefatigable taste. A few apple trees their great-grandmother planted ages ago grew in abundance on the lawn despite never once being tended to by the current generation of Ardeleans. A sign hung above the door – a smiley, ebony haired witch clumsily riding a broomstick with the words "Life's a Witch" dropped below.

And standing outside, with a smirk that could burn wallpaper, was none other than the devil herself.

"Hello little brother," Daciana said as Romy stepped out, her arms crossed, draped in black and smugness. "Welcome home."

They brushed past her to get inside. "Our grandmother just died and you're smiling like a dingo with a baby in its teeth."

She scoffed. "Are you accusing me of having no reverence for our dear, departed High Mage?"

"I'm accusing you of being an asshole. Where's father?"

She pulled at their wrist to stop them from going further. "He's in the study with mother, and they are not to be disturbed."

They pulled their hand away. "I'll be quick."

She activated her Hue with the swiftness of a striking cobra. "*Opri.*"

Their feet froze to the ground, smothered in violet magic.

"*Înceta.*" Their own magenta Hue overwhelmed hers and burned the ice away. "I am talking to father. Stay out of my way."

She glared at them before shaking the battle-lust off her face. "Okay. Go on."

Pleasantly surprised by her sudden shift in impulse control, they turned away and continued down towards their father's study. Beyond the ornate gothic doors, they could hear muffled yelling in Romanian.

'He must be talking with our relatives in Romania…' Second thoughts began to come to mind. 'Is this really a good idea? What if I just end up making everything worse? For me, for him… for everybody…'

Then a third thought, one that rang clearly through their mind in their grandmother's voice. 'You can do this, my love.'

And a fourth, in Nico's voice. 'I will always be here for you.'

With the chorus of support wondrously conquering the voice of their insecurities, Romy pushed their way inside and found their father at his desk while his mother, Angelica, sat in the corner, drinking a strange brew.

Despite her husband clearly having an emotional conversation with whoever was on the phone, Angelica squealed drunk delight at seeing her second born.

"My little Lamb!" She ran to pull them into an ear-popping mom-hug. "Maron! Look! It's your-"

"Quiet!" He roared at his wife before returning to his call.

"Perhaps it's best if we leave him for now… it's been an emotional day for everybody."

"I wonder why," they answered, sarcastically, as they eyeballed their mother's concoction. A strange, thick, gray-ish, brown-ish, soup-like drink with bits of leaves and meat floating about. "What is that stuff?"

"Oh thissh?!" She said with a slur as she gulped some more down. "Boggy's special remedy for heartache and emotional strife. It's a few ginger flakes marinated in lavender, a spoonful or so of oyster mucous, pheasant heart, the hair of the person causing you pain, and three shots of vodka! She calls it-"

Romy could tell where this was going. "Her Hair of the Dog. Yeah, clever. Very… Bogdana."

"I know, right?!" she said with a giggle and a swiggle. "You should say hi to her by the way. I'm sure she missed you."

"No, she didn't. Perhaps you've drunk enough, today, mother."

She put on a pouty face. "Oh, stop. Boggy loves you, you know that."

"She really doesn't. And you know that."

She pretended like she didn't hear them say that. "And who knows when your father will be out and ready to face the world again. We have so much to deal with. The rites alone will be a bitch to arrange. Crones from all over the world are banging down the door to get involved."

The standard coven mage's funeral was an incredibly involved affair with many rituals required. But it was nothing compared to the burial rites of a high mage as powerful and accomplished as Doina Ardelean. The mental gymnastics required to properly organize the seating arrangements without offending any of the guests or their patron Gods was enough to give Romy a migraine.

And then, they realized that if they went through with becoming a hedge, they wouldn't be allowed to attend their Bună's funeral.

Their grandmother's voice returned. 'I believe in you, my love.'

They sighed. "Mom, I need to talk to you and dad, alone, right now."

"Darlin', surely it can-"

"I don't want to see Bogdana, or anybody else."

"Not even Grigori?"

Seeing their younger brother would have been nice, as he was the only member of their family they genuinely loved, but it would also serve to further dismantle their confidence. "Mom, please."

In a flash, her flushed red face turned pale as a realization a lifetime coming dawned on her. "You're goin' to do it, aren't you? Forfeit…"

"Mom. I can't-"

"It's okay." She held back a snob, transfiguring it into a slight sniffle. "Stupid Boggy. The potion only covers so much sadness." She pulled a strand of Romy's hair out.

"Ow!"

And tucked it inside her satchel. "It's just been one of those weeks. We lost Doina. And now I'm goin' to lose you."

"I'm sorry."

"No, you're not. And that's okay. I wouldn't be either." She gave a sad, half-smile. "I wouldn't be either…"

It was then that Romy saw a dark glint in her eyes. As if in this brief moment, she silently recognized her child's suffering for the first time in their shared life. "Mom-"

The study door burst open and an exhausted Maron, newly anointed as the Ardelean High Mage, fell onto the two.

"This fuckin' day!" He said as he put all of his weight on his wife and child. "Ugh… Lamb! You have no idea how happy I am to see you!"

He lifted Romy up into a bear hug that only a large Eastern European man such as he could accomplish. His mother's death had clearly made him more sentimental. Affection from their father was rare and when expressed could be very intense. So much so that a single hug could make Romy forget why they felt so alone and afraid in the coven. It almost made them forget why they were visiting in the first place. Almost.

"I forfeit Coven, blood, and bond," they said in the most unmistakably serious tone.

Maron's face fell faster than an unprepared baby bird. He released Romy from his embrace and, with a grave sense of disappointment in his voice, activated his sapphire blue Hue and recited the admonition. *"Go, hedge, and find no home in the Ardelean Coven, nor any other Coven in this world."*

Romy spared no time in running out of the house like a bat out of hell. Their mother quietly drank her drink while their father turned back into his office and slammed the door shut.

They ran past Daciana, who, unfortunately, had nothing better to do than ask, "Leaving so soon, little brother?"

"Yeah. For good."

Bewildered, she started following them to their car. "What?"

"I revoked the coven. I'm out."

"Excuse me???"

"You heard me. I'm not your *'little brother'* anymore, so you can feel free to stop calling me that. I'm a hedge now. Bye."

They were about to open their car door before a blast of flame beat their hand to the handle.

They turned back towards her, furious. "What the actual fuck is wrong with you?"

"What the fuck is wrong with *you*? You're going to just leave our coven hours after our high mage passed on? Abandon us, just like that?"

"She wasn't just the high mage, you garbage dope! Bună was the only person who made me feel like I belonged here. She never threw fireballs at me, for one. She never tortured me, or belittled me, or made me feel like shit."

"Perhaps if you didn't behave like shit-"

Losing control, they activated their Hue and hurled a bolt of SoulSpark that hit her in the face, leaving a terribly deep cut down through her left eye.

She screamed. "How dare you?!"

Her fingers glowed a violent violet and she released a laser of pure heat. In one clean maneuver, Romy's hands were sliced off at the wrist. They heard their cousin, David, screaming as he ran towards them.

"You're running out of steam, Daciana. Surrender." They were riding a terrifying high that they had never felt before in battle.

They would never admit it aloud, but this fight had pulled something out of them. Something addicting in its awesome beauty and power. Ever more so addicting was the lust for vengeance on behalf of the abused child still crying for help deep within their heart.

Though she would never admit it, Daciana was at the end of her rope and running out of ideas. And, in that moment, she could only think of one.

"Fine… I surrender," she said as she deactivated her hue.

Romy was so confused, their eyes nearly crossed. "The fuck you do."

"I surrender. I'll talk."

They quickly saw through the ruse. "I know about the Covenant, Daciana. If you talk, you die. If you surrender, you're going to jail, and we're going to rip what we need to know outta your head."

She was out of breath. She couldn't keep up the fight. "Seems I have no choice," she said with a convincing sigh.

'Better safe than sorry,' they said to themselves as they stretched out their hands to cast a binding spell.

Seeing her opportunity, she quickly activated her Hue and sent a laser of pure heat at their hands, slicing them at the wrist. The wound was instantaneously cauterized by the heat of the very beam that opened it.

They thought they were screaming but they couldn't hear anything. The world around them had gone silent. The shock was setting in. Their mind was turning off.

Every synapse in their brain was firing on all cylinders. Their nerves were flaring like a meteor shower entering the Earth's atmosphere. They felt like they were about to vomit. Their chest tightened around their lungs and heart. And then it exploded.

But their heart did not come out. Something else did. Something powerful.

A long staff. Roughly as tall as Romy. The head appeared to be a small-scale replica of the universe itself, represented as a grand metallic mobile. Glimmers of stars floated about within it. Mysterious and beautiful, it felt strange but familiar. Like a long-lost friend. A pair of eyes that have always been watching them, only to find out they were your own and yet still a stranger's.

They reached out to touch it and were so flabbergasted they hadn't even realized that their hands had mysteriously grown back. They held it and, for the first time in their life, they felt complete.

And then they were gone. In a void, black as space. Stars filled the vast expanse of emptiness, slowly illuminating it. But upon closer inspection, they were not stars but faces. People. People they knew.

And then they were back. In the real world. And Daciana was at their feet. And Guy was standing before them, asking them if they were okay.

And then a flash of light.

And then nothing.

13

A Grave Undertaking

"We are so fucked," was the best Kass could throw out. She was dazed, confused, full of self-loathing for not being able to save her best friend in time, but also determined and full of confidence that she could recover them.

She was hugging him. She was happy to see him. And even happier to know he was going to be moving into Nico's old office and take his place in their home. She was also concerned about Romy's emotional security. She would later vocalize this in private, unaware that Alfie could hear her through the paper-thin walls.

"No, we're not," Nico sternly responded. He was as he usually was: cold, calculating, distancing himself emotionally from the stressful situation he was being placed in, and trying hard not to overthink while simultaneously overthinking. Overthinking about Romy, their relationship, the world at large, their family, and everything in between.

He had called ahead. He had left several of his things behind and wanted them back. He scheduled a time. Romy, understandably, was not present. Kass was hoping to answer the door, but Alfie got there first. Nico radiated awkward, isolated energy at the sight of his own replacement welcoming him into his old home. All he ever said to Alfie was "Hi," and "Bye." Kass, meanwhile, had several words for Nico. Most of them were four-lettered.

"Actually, you quite are," Ianto said with a smart smirk that was so confident one would almost forget that he was shackled in chains of ice. Nico's design. His vampiric nature ensured that all of his feelings would be blocked from Alfie's extra-sensory skills. Yet Alfie still knew his brother. Despite being undead, he was still a child who used his shroud of confidence to hide his eagerness to escape.

He was screaming at Alfie to run as they tried to escape the horde of Vampire gangsters chasing after them. His brother kept screaming at him to run and hide. His brother kept radiating fear, concern, and hope that their parents would hear him scream and come rescue them. His brother kept feeling, until he stopped. And Alfie could not feel him anymore. A vision he would rather forget but his photographic and eidetic memory – triggered, haphazardly, by any extreme emotional stimulation – prevented him from pursuing this dream.

To say their "chance reunion" had jarred him would have been a grandiose understatement. Alfie was flabbergasted beyond words. The statistical odds of a London-based gang of

Vampires traveling to the States to help a villainous coven of necromancers, led by their roommate's family, were staggeringly low.

Alfie made the calculations in his mind as his companions rambled amongst themselves about "tactical thinking" and "we should take the fight to them." He thought of all the sunlight Ianto and his friends would have had to have avoided on their sojourn to the states. Unable to obtain proper passports, they would have been forced to take some sort of freighter, travelling on the lowest deck to avoid the sun.

He thought of all the times Ianto would protect Alfie from bullies. He thought about watching as Ianto was feasted on by a trio of vampires, while their leader attempted to consume his blood. Finding extraterrestrial hemoglobin to his disliking, he spat it out and kicked Alfie in the face, knocking him unconscious. When he awoke in a hospital bed a day later, his mother tearfully told him that Ianto was gone forever. Soon after, they started hearing news reports of a gang of vampires being led by a young blond boy, wreaking havoc across the Atlantic border.

He thought of Romy.

"Did anybody else see the staff?" Alfie asked the still arguing group.

Kass looked at him quizzically. "What staff, Alfie?" She was confused and concerned that perhaps Alfie was seeing things. Worse yet, she was concerned that she had missed an important detail that could lead to solving the mystery.

In the corner of his eye, he saw Ianto smirk.

"The staff Romy was holding before they disappeared, along with Guy and Daciana, just now."

"They weren't holding a staff, Alfie," Nico said, matter-of-factly. He was feeling annoyed that Alfie would bring up something he felt was inconsequential. And also guilty for feeling annoyed because he figured Alfie was just trying to be helpful, but more so he was scared for Romy's well-being. And thinking of Romy made his heart hurt.

"Yes, they were. Ianto saw it too. Most likely because, as a Vampire, he too is immune to magic and – in this instance – an immensely powerful memory charm."

They all turned to Ianto, whose smirk became even more smug than before. "It was very pretty, would you not say so yourself, brother?"

"Indeed. Though I have seen it before, this is the first time I have witnessed it manifest so prodigiously. So, to confirm, the only people present capable of perceiving the staff Romy conjures whenever they are in mortal danger are those immune to magic?"

Nico and Kass just looked at one another. Kass was oozing curiosity and the struggle one feels when left out of an important loop. Nico just became more annoyed, this time at the magic he feels is responsible for so much suffering, particularly his own. And once again, he felt guilty for being annoyed.

Alfie made a mental note, *'Offer Nico counseling services and compare schedules once zombie apocalypse over and friends rescued.'*

"So, you've seen the staff before?" Kass asked, her curiosity and desire to fight superseding her confusion and fear.

"Yes, once or twice while assisting Romy with their various exorcistic endeavors. In fact, I most recently spied it yesterday. It was quite a sight. It is unfortunate you cannot see it for yourself."

Nico became more frustrated. And then he became angry. He pulled some ice from Ianto's bonds and formed them around his fist. He held up the icy gauntlet to Ianto's face in a threatening pose.

"What is it?" He asked with venom practically spraying from his mouth. "The staff? What is it? And why do they want it so badly?"

"Do you honestly think I am intimidated by you, you incredibly tiny man?"

An icy spike extended towards his neck. "I want answers, bloodsucker. Spill."

He snickered. "Is this your idea of being the bad cop?"

"No, this is," Kass said as she casually walked over and kicked in Ianto's knee until it bent sideways.

"AAAAARRGGGGGHHH!" He screamed. "Fucking fuuuuck!"

"I wonder how long it'll take before those vampy healing abilities kick in?" She said with an incredible swagger. The true bad cop. "How about you answer those questions my friend asked you before I start ripping off your toenails, one by one?"

"Alright, fine!" He shouted. "It is called the Demiurge. Ancient artifact of great magic. Passed down from generation to generation, blah blah blah, stereotypical magical weapon bullshit."

"Demiurge?" Nico's cold mind suddenly warmed with thoughts and matriculations. He began to search the hallways of his mental palace for any mention of this word before, like a human google.

"Aye, the Demiurge. Rumor has it, your little boyfriend…"

"They're not a boy, or my boyfriend, they're my ex-**partner** and you will not misgender them **again**."

"Fine. Your little *ex-partner* owns this super powerful weapon. Capable of incredible feats of magic."

Nico's eyes widened as he beheld a eureka moment. "The Demiurge. I remember it now!"

"Remember what?" Kass asked.

"Elementary mythology. The Demiurges were four weapons used by humanity to seal the Gods into the Spirit World. Some people think that if they could be brought back together it would usher in the return of the Gods. Kass, this explains so much."

"Yeah, it totally does," she lied as she allowed her confusion to reclaim control. "Like what?"

"Like how Romy, despite not really being a battlemage, can go toe to toe with someone like Daciana without breaking a sweat. Or how, whenever things seem like they're about to go south and everyone's going to die, all of a sudden Romy saves the day."

Kass just stared at him. "When has Romy ever saved the day?"

"A plethora of times," Alfie interjected. "Though, to be fair, you probably were made to forget the events that occurred due to the memory charm."

"That is strange," Nico said. "Do you think Romy's the one who cast the charm?"

"I do not believe so. It affects them as well. So, it stands to reason that they did not. They have no clue about the staff as far as I know. I have been studying the mind of Romy for many years now and never have they ever shown that they were aware of their true power."

Kass looked at him with an estranged expression. "You've been studying Romy's mind?"

"Of course, I have. It is an incredibly fascinating one to say the least."

A fat crunch and a disgusting squish signaled that Ianto's knee had been stuck back into place. "I hate when I do that."

"Why do they want it?" Kass asked.

"Some great big hooey spell of theirs. Fuck if I know. It is a powerful weapon, they are power hungry psychopaths, thus they want it… badly."

"That was helpful," Kass said, radiating a strong desire to hit him harder, in a much more sensitive spot.

"I told you already, I do not know much. You should be happy I have anything to offer in the first place."

Alfie looked deep into his brother's eyes. A pool of black sclera surrounding a blood red iris. "Ianto. Please. Take us to Romy."

Ianto looked right back into Alfie's glowing pink eyes. "How much?"

"Ugh," Nico groaned. "'*How much?*' You want money? In exchange for our friend's life?"

"Exactly. How much?"

"Just two," Kass said.

Ianto's face scrunched in confusion. "Two?"

Kass kicked Ianto right in the seat of his pants, hitting him with all of her strength. "FOR ALL THAT IS UNHOLY, WHAT THE FUCK!"

"You get to keep your balls, you blood sucking, pre-pubescent bitch boy," Kass said. "I'm not here for this 'play your cards right' bullshit. I'm here to save my best friend and, if you didn't notice, an entire city. Cut the games and take us to Romy. *Now*."

"And Guy," Alfie reminded her.

Her irritation increased. "Yes, and Guy. Take us to Romy *and* Guy."

He sighed. "Fine. But you are not going to like where you are bound to go."

She gestured to the fire and rubble in their midst. "Look around, boo. I am surrounded by things I don't like. I have learned to live with them. But can you live an eternal life without your balls?"

Nico's ears perked like a curious cat. "That's actually a very interesting question. Could you?"

"I would rather not find out thank you." Ianto's face was giving away his desperation to escape with all of his parts intact. Something he was willing to betray his benefactors for. Alfie couldn't feel it, but he could see it. He believed his brother. "Fine, I shall take you to their little lair."

"Where is it?" Kass asked.

"Five miles south of here and about two hundred feet below us."

Her eye twitched with gross concern. "What do you mean?"

"Your friends are being kept in the depths of the sewers. An underground bomb shelter that was destroyed by an earthquake decades ago. Excavated by the mages. Now accessible only by traveling along several meters of raw, dirty sewage." He smiled with all of his razor-sharp teeth.

"Ugh," Kass said to herself. "Nico, you wouldn't happen to know any 'anti-smell' spells, would you?"

Alfie's mind did not work like everybody else's. Obviously. He was an alien in possession of powerful empathic abilities. Being within a few feet of somebody caused him to channel their emotions, whether he wanted to or not. And because his parents had issues with boundaries, he oft expressed the alienating habit of verbalizing whatever he was feeling whenever he was feeling it. This helped him sort between his own emotions and the para-empathic ones. However, it also hindered his social skills.

His entire existence made him a natural target for bullying by children in the various neighborhoods he grew up in. His family was forced to move multiple times for multiple reasons. Alfie was "causing disruptions" so they had to transfer schools. Alfie was constantly being physically assaulted and the family was getting death threats, so they had to leave the village. Alfie needed a special American tutor to help him hone his talents, so they had to leave the country.

Yet throughout all the hardships, he always had Ianto. He had his talent for all-in-good-fun mischief that kept Alfie from being too cerebral and staying too long in his head (as well as other peoples'). He had his friendship. His willingness to spend time with his younger brother despite their four-year age difference. His patience in showing Alfie how to play video games that helped teach him to focus his mind and turn off his powers. It was through his brother that he was able to truly take control and develop into the powerful psychic he inevitably became.

He often remembers the time he asked Ianto, "You never get frustrated by me. Why?"

"What do you mean?"

"Frustration radiates around everybody I meet whenever I enter the room. My very appearance causes disturbance. This only compounds with the frustration people feel when I use my powers. But you never get frustrated with me. Why not?"

Ianto smiled at him. "When I was just about four years old, dad and I went camping in the backyard. We saw a shooting star and Dad told me to make a wish. I closed my eyes and wished with all my heart, 'Please send me a little brother.' And that shooting star listened, went to your planet, picked you up and brought you home."

Alfie smiled. He would later learn that this was nowhere near what actually happened.

On Planet Nine, empathic powers are considered a genetic aberration, little more than a disease that affected 0.001% of the population. A disease that was controlled and treated by adopting the child off world.

Alfie was devastated when he found out this hard truth, but Ianto was steadfast in his love and kindness.

"Their loss is our gain! You are the best person I know, and I am so happy that you are my brother!"

It was this kind of memory that Alfie would cling to whenever he was forced to deal with the reality that his once loving brother had been transformed into a selfish, flesh-eating demon. The kind of demon that wouldn't think twice about joining a villainous pack of witches in assaulting an entire city. As well as double-crossing them in order to save himself.

This knowledge weighed heavier on Alfie's heart than the sewage weighed on his shoes as they were led by Ianto through the strangely spacious utility tunnels. The bare breath utility lights only just illuminated their shit-filled path. He would need to spend at least three days in the shower to feel clean again.

"How much longer, Ianto?" He asked.

"Another mile or so… I believe… Maybe?" Ianto was held by a pair of icy cuffs that were held by a psionic rope attached to Nico's mind. "I am doing this all based on the memory I have of visiting their little lair once about three weeks ago. So, pardon any missteps."

Kass was less than comforted by this. "Reminder to all: I am doing this *barefoot*, so there will be *no missteps!* Thank you."

"Why are you barefoot, again, miss?" an honestly curious Ianto asked.

"Ugh… it is not my job to enlighten you about my people and their combat methods."

"But… surely, it is disgusting to be-"

"Yes, it is, motherfucker, so guide us faster!"

"Of course, madame."

Then, they all heard a low, grunting, growling noise.

This turned Kass's stomach. "Oh, for fuck's sake. Please don't tell me…"

But her suspicions were confirmed moments later when an avalanche of zombies appeared. A vanguard for the wicked Ardeleans. Nico, unimpressed, merely lifted his hands and used the sewer water to part the sea of undead, freezing them in a blink. This had the fortunate bonus of removing the brown, tarnished water from around their feet.

"Awesome!" Kass said. However, it didn't take long for the wheels in her brain to start turning. "Wait… couldn't you have done that *before*, Nico?"

"Honestly, by the time I stopped being disgusted long enough to remember I could move water with my mind, I was too embarrassed – and scared – to bring it up."

"So, you just let me walk in shit?"

"I'm sorry, but at least we're getting close. Right?"

"Sure," Ianto said with a Vampire's grin.

"You are personally washing my feet when we're done with this, Nico."

They kept walking, stopping every so often to re-kill a zombie, with the numbers getting smaller and smaller as it became clear they were getting to the source.

As they turned a corner, Nico spied something scribed on the wall. A strange symbol.

"Anti-detection rune. Keeps them from being found by magical means. Put up enough and you're invisible to the magical world. Must be why MIST couldn't see this coming. Usually, we can catch large congregations of mages before they try to kill everybody."

"What happens if we erase it?" Kass asked.

"You weaken the magic." She bared her claws and slashed at the mark. "There's probably dozens more, Kass."

"Then if you see a mark, you slash it. Hopefully we get at least a couple reinforcements as we face what should be a dozen necromancers. You see a rune, you wipe it."

"Agreed." Nico stretched out his hand and mentally threw all the water into a forward whirlwind, power washing the walls of the sewer in a single wipe. "If there are any left in this corridor, I will also give you a pedicure. Deal?"

"My eyesight is better than yours, water boy. I'll hold you to it."

"Can we please get this all over with? I am literally freezing my hands off." Ianto complained as he shook his icy cuffs. "I think we should only be a few meters away. A small clave behind a big door."

They walked down the way to a large door thick enough to resist an atomic bomb blast. Nico activated his ice blue Hue and recited an Italian incantation. *"Oltre la magia, aperto per me."* However, nothing happened. He repeated himself. *"Oltre la magia, aperto per me."* Still nothing. "Shit. Their resistance runes must be covering the walls, I can't open it."

"Well, how about this?" Kass walked up to the door and tried turning the doorknob, but it felt like it was glued stuck with concrete. "Okay, why did I think that would work?"

"Cuz you believe in the bright side of life. We're gonna have to do some drilling." Nico prepared to summon a great blade of ice from the sewer water, only for Ianto to interject.

"Or you could let me say the password," the Vampire touched his dead, cold hands to the door. "Password."

The door opened with a massive creak to a great fire-ball that the four of them barely dodged. When the smoke had cleared, the villainous coven stood before them. A small militia that outnumbered the rescue team two to one. And Daciana was at the head of the pack.

Her love for dramatics could not fail her as she quoted the Brothers' Grimm. "Nibble, nibble like a mouse. Who is nibbling at my house? It seems we have some intruders who need to be dealt with. In fact, I think it was you," she pointed right at Kass. "Half-breed, who murdered my coven sister. You're going to burn for that."

Alfie, Kass, and Nico all looked at each other with bewildered eyes, but they knew that this fight was coming. And mentally, they all had prepared for it.

"Incredible self-assurance and unmatched bravery," Alfie said as he read the room. "As Kass would say: Bring it."

And Kass had to add: "… Bitch."

14

Wake

"Please," An almond-skinned woman with dark hair and even darker eyes pleaded to a warlock dressed in a blood red cloak. Once upon a time, she was healthy and full of life, but her recent ordeals had left her a thinned shell of who she once was. "You exorcised the demon! Make it give us back our son! Please!"

A seven-year-old boy was tucked into his red race car bed just a few feet away. Eyes closed. Face pale. Dead.

The magician spoke in a dark, weathered voice. Grated, like a rusty door closing on a sunny day. "The boy has been claimed by the Spirit that possessed this house. It demanded payment and took your son in the exchange."

"Our son's soul was not for sale!" The boy's father shouted. His blue eyes flashed through his clouded, horn-rimmed glasses. "Bring him back! You gave up his soul, you get it back!"

"I apologize if the circumstances of our transaction did not align with your expectations, but there is no returning a soul from the Aether once it has been claimed. Flesh wounds can be healed, but they are nothing compared to a knife to the soul."

The boy's mother fell to the ground. "Please. *Please.*" She begged through terrible tears. "We'll do anything. Please."

The man in red smiled. "There is something."

"What?" The desperate woman asked, too dehydrated to continue crying. She wanted to fall to the floor, but her legs were frozen in place.

The warlock could sense her anguish. "I can bring your son back-"

"Yes?!" She quickly blurted out without thinking.

"But his soul will forever be latched to mine." He spoke slowly, with a grated seriousness. He stood tall, emanating a commanding presence. "He will live but by my will alone. He will breathe, and laugh, and grow into what I assume will be a fine gentleman. But one day, I will ask him to pay the true price for his resurrection."

"And what would that be?"

"Something you need not worry about for ages to come. Only know that until I die, he will be a part of me and I a part of him. He will be alive. But he will be mine."

The two looked at one another, wordlessly discussing the warlock's bargain amongst themselves.

"Is there no other way?" The father asked with a weak voice.

"It is the only way."

Their sad eyes joined together once more. In the end, they decided that a son bound forever to a stranger's soul was better than a dead one.

"Do it," he said in a dark voice.

"Then it is a deal. I will bring your son back."

"Oh, thank you." The mother's face began to beam like the sun.

"The circumstances of the spell require it to be a secret to all, including the child. But know that no true harm will come to your son. He will be the Bane of Death, so mote it be by the blessing of my Lord."

"Just do it," the hopeless woman commanded.

The Necromancer walked over to the dead child, lying on his bed. He pulled out an athame, a ceremonial dagger, with Hellish runes inscribed on the blade.

"If you must bear witness, do so without word or action. I must perform deeds that will most definitely cause stress upon your faint hearts. But know that it is the only way to bring your son back to life."

The two grieving, frantic parents held onto each other and nodded.

The warlock slashed his own palm, releasing a flow of blood that he wiped on the child's face. He then forcibly opened the boy's dead yet still bright blue eyes and allowed the blood to trickle into his sockets as he summoned his magic from within himself. Creating a dark red Hue around his body as he did so. He knelt before the blood-soaked child and began to mutter his spell, inaudible to all in the room as the red light enveloped the boy. He began to levitate. The blood covering his face quickly seeped into his very pores.

The man ceased his chanting and the boy descended back down onto the bed. The man then propped open the boy's mouth and began to perform CPR.

A sterile half-minute later, the boy gasped for air. His pale skin returned to its normal sun-kissed state.

He was alive.

He looked up at the strange man, and with his first new breath asked, "Who are you?"

15

In Memoriam

Guy woke up tied to a chair, facing a blank, grey, cement wall with no memory of how he got there. His hands and feet were tightly bound, no wiggle room.

'Well, this is fun.'

He looked around and tried to reflect on how, in such a short amount of time, he found himself in such a predicament. He started thanking whatever God made him incapable of dying. "At least I can be confident," He thought aloud just to cut the silence.

"Guy?" A familiar voice responded from behind.

"Romy? Are you also tied up or am I *really* bad at picking sexual partners?"

"Yeah, I'm bound... like Jennifer Tilly."

"Big fan of nineties, erotic, lesbian thrillers?"

"I'm so happy I'm with someone who gets that reference."

They laughed through the fear they were both feeling.

"How exactly did we get here? Last thing I remember was getting between you and your sister."

"I have vague memories of that as well. Mostly I just remember kicking my sister's ass. Which was awesome."

"It really was. Excellent job, B-T-dubs."

"Thank you. Thank you. Hold your applause, I'm just an ordinary person, kicking ass and taking names like the boss ass bitch that I am." They laughed again. "My main question is: if I won the fight, how did we get here? I feel like winning usually comes hand in hand with *not* getting captured and tied up."

"Yeah, I don't remember that happening either. I do remember a big flash of light."

"Same! And maybe getting hit with a stick? I'm shaky on the details."

"You know what the weirdest part about this is?"

"What?"

"Not my worst second date."

Romy laughed through their nose. "Oh, that's depressingly hilarious. I don't know what's worse, that you consider *this* a second date or that a combination zombie apocalypse, family reunion from hell, finding out you're technically dead, and getting kidnapped doesn't qualify as the worst second date you've ever had."

"I've had some doozies. And even worse hook-ups. One time, this dude stopped in the middle of sex to tell me he wanted me to smile more."

"EWWWW!" Romy would've jumped out of their chair if they could.

"I know right! What's the worst date you've ever been on?"

"I've only technically been on two dates in my life. My first date with Nico and my first date with you. But, I guess, if this counts as a date…"

"I totally get it. What about worst hookup? I remember when I topped for the first time, and I got you-know-what on my you-know-where."

"Oh, that's sexy."

Guy sighed. "Yeah, suffice it to say, there's a reason why I usually bottom."

"Admittedly, I've only bottomed like five times in my life."

"Not a fan?"

"I've found that I need to trust someone significantly before I can give them something so precious as my little treasure box. Also, douching is a unique artform I have never been able to fully master. And I'm incredibly insecure about how flat my ass is."

Guy laughed. "I happen to like your flat ass. Also, I thought you've only ever dated Nico."

"Yeah, but I hooked up with a lot of rando's before mustering the courage to ask him out. And we opened ourselves up here and there. Sorta depended on our mood. Usually I'm a one-person-at-a-time kind of person. I'm not ashamed to say I'm generally 'monogamish.' But boss ass bitches can get very horny."

"Understandable. When I'm single, I'm a slut. When I'm with someone, I'm with them and them alone… Unless…"

"Unless? Unless what?"

"Unless they're terrible in bed. I love to have sex, and I love to have sex well. Is that so wrong?"

"Amen, ho. I'd fist bump you if I could. Or maybe kiss you if you'd consent."

Guy smiled with a candied sweetness. "Oh, I'd consent. I'd consent big time. And Romy?"

"Yeah?"

"For what it's worth, whatever happens today, I'm really happy I got to meet you."

"Gosh, why are you so perfect?"

"Why do you deflect nice comments?"

"Because I have self-esteem problems. Which is ironic to say the least."

"Why is it ironic?"

"My Focus is Confidence, right?"

"Sure." Guy still didn't have the greatest understanding as to what all went into using magic, but he didn't want to distract Romy when they clearly had something they wanted to get off their chest.

"Well, I'm only truly *confident* when I use magic. Everything else, I have to fight myself to feel like I'm not complete and utter shit."

"You're not shit, Romy."

"Ain't I? I suck at pretty much all kinds of basic human stuff. Like love and communication and kindness and happiness. Even in my happiest moments with Nico, or Kass, or anybody, there's always been this loneliness. This emptiness. This void. I've always felt less than everyone else."

"'Less than' in what way?"

"Like… incomplete?"

"And I would bet you'd love to figure out why," a gravely, almost stereotypically sinister voice said from the shadows.

"Who's that? Who's there?" Romy asked the darkness.

"A friend. Someone closer to the both of you in more ways than either of you could ever understand." The voice stepped into the light where both Guy and Romy could see him.

"Councilman Proctor?" Romy said in disbelief. "Really? The only mage on the city council is the bad guy? That's depressing. Is this one of those 'absolute power corrupts absolutely' deals?"

"Is this one of those 'I'm going to keep talking to hide my fear and shame' deals?" He fired back.

It almost shut them up. "Touché. Speak freely."

"Thank you. Such a pleasure. I understand that I'm the villain in this situation. And I know how cliché it is for the villain to dramatically monologue about his diabolical plan to his victims. But the spell I plan on enacting tonight requires everyone involved to be aware of everything and anything that has gone into it."

Romy's brown eyes flared with knowledge. "A 'power in truth' spell? That's some primeval magic you're going for, bro."

Guy had so many questions. "Wait. Wait. Weren't you all burnt up a couple hours ago?"

"I'm a mage. I made a glamour."

"What's that?"

"It's an illusion," Romy informed him.

"Oh.. okay... sorry for interrupting."

Proctor's face twisted in confusion at him. "Anyway, I think it's best to start at the beginning."

"A very good place to start," Romy sang as Guy snickered.

Proctor cleared his throat with a severe level of passive aggression. "While my name is legally Randall Proctor, my true name is Henry Tooth."

"Henry Tooth?" Romy said with the taste of confusion stuck on their tongue. "I can understand your desire to change it. That's not exactly the most villainous name in the world."

"But Proctor doesn't scream 'villain' either," Guy said.

"That is true."

"Are you two quite finished? Because I'm not."

Romy's eye twinkled impishly. "The sooner you tell us everything, the sooner I assume we die. So, I'm not exactly in a hurry to go along with this bullshit."

"Well, you have no choice, anyway… where was I?"

Guy could not help but answer his question. "Your real name is Henry Tooth."

"Thank you. Anyway, I was born in 1634 and-"

"Wait, the fuck did you just say?" Romy was flabbergasted.

"Yeah, for real, who is your plastic surgeon? Remind me to call them when I'm your age. If I make it that far. Althhough, I did find out that I'm immortal today."

"But you still age," Romy noted.

"Yeah, I do, what's up with that?"

"Will the two of you shut up? For all that is unholy on this Earth, it is like talking to a couple of chickens."

"Fun fact: chicken is actually British slang for a young homosexual," Guy said with a smile that could light up a galaxy.

Tooth/Proctor was about as amused as a crocodile at the dentist. "Why did it have to be the two of you? Why, Guy Garrison, did you have to be the one that I bless with my shared immortality?"

Romy gasped, even though they had already deduced this. "You made him a Revenant? Why?"

"I'm literally about to explain that. Anyway, in sixteen-sixty-two, the Witch War began in Salem when a crew of Puritans executed several innocent witches simply for existing. The war lasted for a year, during which hundreds of people on both sides perished."

"Yes, thank you for the history lesson, Father Exposition. Could you skip to the main point?"

"The tide turned in our favor when famed battle mage Beatrix Bishop stepped into the fray. Beatrix also wielded a special weapon we call the Demiurge."

"Demiurge?" Guy had to ask.

"It's an ancient weapon," Romy responded. "Mythology says it was a gift from the Gods."

"History. Not mythology. Four traitorous, heathen Gods fought against their own brethren to *'save humanity.'* They gave us four gifts – a sword, an amulet, a chalice, and a staff. And this staff has had countless names, Merlin's Staff, Chronos' Scythe, the Caduceus. But the name that has stuck with it the longest is the Demiurge. And what's unique about this staff, amongst all four of the Heathen Gods' gifts, is that it is said to be attached to the very soul of the mage who first wielded it. A soul cursed to be reincarnated lifetime after lifetime, forever kept from joining the Aether."

Romy realized that they had to function as a translator for the non-magical Guy and gave an explanation. "The Aether is the magical afterlife. Also known as the realm of the Gods."

"Thank you."

"This soul would eventually reincarnate as Beatrix Bishop, who refused to use the Demiurge for its true purpose – reuniting us with the Gods. The Totems of the Traitorous Gods, when brought together, could be used to rip open the walls between our mortal plane and the Aether itself. We could bring back our otherworldly masters, and mages would once again reign supreme over humanity."

"Or the Gods would go nuts again, like they did before, and everybody – mage and mortal – would be enslaved. Cuz history, as you may know considering you are a billion years old, has a way of repeating itself."

"Did that really happen?" Guy asked.

"The Judeo-Christian machine that runs most of the modern educational system doesn't *want* you to know it happened, but it happened." Romy explained. "A couple hundred millennia ago, our world was ruled over by Gods whose power was fueled by our emotions. It created the Aether, which granted some members of humanity magic. But the Gods became power hungry and treated humanity like cattle. There was a rebellion, millions were slaughtered, so a small collective of Heathen Gods created the-"

Tooth cut them off. "Totems. Could you please stop interrupting me?!"

"Dude, it's not my fault you are the least compelling monologist I've ever met in my life."

"Yeah, for real, you are lacking the kind of grandiose passion one might expect from a villain explaining his master plan."

"That's because I don't actually *want* to do this. I *need* to do this. There is a massive difference."

"Just skip to the main point, Toothache. What does all of this have to do with me and Guy?"

"You are Beatrix's reincarnation, you idiot!"

Romy gasped again. "Shut up!"

"For the love of- I told Beatrix that we should use her power to summon a God and use its power to wipe out our enemies, but she refused."

"But only all four of the Totems could be used to open the Aether."

"Permanently open, yes. But one is perfectly capable of tearing open the veil long enough to summon one very specific deity on its own. She used the power of the Demiurge, instead, to cast a World Law spell-"

Romy craned their head so Guy could hear them say, "A World Law spell is a spell that affects the world at large. Sorta like the one keeping mages from being able to make their own money. Usually requires a lot of magic."

Tooth/Proctor continued. "A World Law spell that made everyone forget that the staff even existed in the first place. The only reason I'm immune is because my Unspoken Word – Memoriam – allows me to inhale the unfiltered and uncensored memories of the dead. She then sacrificed her very life to end the war, becoming a martyr and saving us all from mutually assured destruction. But she also imprisoned us in the cataclysmic failure that is the Coven system. We became a broken people. And I plan on bringing us back. I plan on granting us the salvation that Beatrix re-"

"Blah, blah, fucking blah, you said that I'm Beatrix's reincarnation, right?"

"Ugh… yes…"

"Then how come I've never, ever used or seen this staff you think that I have?"

"I can tell you, most assuredly, that you have. Daciana granted me permission to visit your grandmother's grave. Using my power, I could see through her eyes that, in her presence, you used the staff twice before immediately forgetting about it. I believe yet another side effect of Beatrix's spell is even the wielder is incapable of being aware of its presence until fully activating its power."

"But where is it, though?"

"It's attached to your soul, you fool. It manifests when you need it most. For instance, when you're in mortal danger."

"So, you're telling me that I've-"

"You know exactly what I've told you, so shut up! I intend on using your very essence to summon the Demiurge and tear a hole in the Aether to summon a demon God named Abaddon. There! I said it! Now, moving swiftly onward."

"How did you become immortal?" asked Guy, with the important questions.

Tooth/Proctor sighed in anguish. "I did a sojourn to Egypt where I discovered a self-mummification spell. I no longer have any lungs, or kidneys, but I can't die of old age or illness. It's actually very helpful."

"Really?" Romy pondered. "It's that simple? Huh... I wonder why more people don't do it."

"It's actually not as simple as I make it sound. I had to perform surgery on myself in a crypt under the light of a blood moon. It's very complicated. Anyway, I needed a new body to place Abaddon's soul into."

"Why not your own?" Romy asked before realizing. "Ohhhh…"

Guy was lost. "What? What did I miss?"

"If I summon Abaddon and allow him to possess me, I stand a chance of losing myself in the process. If I allow Abaddon to possess Guy, and then take over Guy's body myself then I will possess the power of a God. So, I started collecting Revenants. Every few decades or so, I create a Revenant in order to stay ready for cornering the Demiurge. However, it's difficult as I am ageless and Revenants do in fact age, even if they never die. So, I usually release them after a few decades."

"Release them?" Guy asked.

"He severs the magic between himself and the Revenant, killing them in the process."

"Really? That's screwed up, dude."

"I don't care what you think!" He sharply said before taking a deep breath and returning to his train of thought. "One day, in my travels, I came upon a small family in California who needed help ridding themselves of a poltergeist who had taken possession of their son. I expelled the poltergeist, but, as I planned, Guy died in the process."

"I'm so happy my death was so convenient for you," Guy said, oozing with passive aggression. "I thought I was some special 'chosen one' immortal dude, like you picked me for a reason. But it turns out, I was just anybody? You suck. It's like I've spent three years in a relationship just to find out I have nothing in common with the person."

"You are an idiot," Tooth said as softly and calmly as possible. "Anyway, a few years ago, I came upon a small coven of Necromancers known as the Ardeleans. One of whom, David, possesses the power to see hidden things. Including the very Demiurge I had been seeking for centuries."

"David…." Romy's heart cracked under the pressure of even the mere mention of their cousin.

"It didn't take much to sway the foolish, younger mages to see how allying with me would benefit them in the coming years. I would summon a God, claim its power, and rule over the world with them as my lieutenants. Everybody wins. Except, of course, the ungifted wastes."

"Really?" Romy, with a greater than standard level of boredom, blurted out. "That's it? World domination? You spent hundreds of years crawling the Earth, collecting immortal baggage, accumulating bad karma, and trying to steal the powers of the Demiurge just to conquer humanity? How basic."

"I spent hundreds of years mourning hundreds of lives whose names the very humanity you think to protect erased from the annals of history. Buried in unmarked graves because they were not strong enough to protect themselves. In my world order, no mage will ever fear that fate."

"No mage needs to fear that fate in the current world order. The Witch Wars are over. The Covens are self-governed, and the hedge mages are protected by MIST."

"If that's what you truly believe, young hedge, then you are far more naive than I originally assumed. You have no idea what the wastes are planning. You have no idea what is in the offing. Ever since the Witch Wars ended in a 'draw,' both sides have worked tirelessly to conceal their true intentions. Yet, indeed, a second war is inevitable. Better to end it before it begins."

"Can I say something?" Guy requested.

"I don't know, *can* you?" He said, obviously to be petty.

Romy groaned in disgust. "Ugh, he's basic *and* pedantic. How can he be my first archenemy?"

Guy continued, nonplussed. "As a licensed therapist, I think this whole scheme is a reflection of your own internalized inferiority complex. Which, clearly, has morphed into a God Complex that, I think, with the proper course of counseling, medications, and treatments – maybe an empath or two – could be resolved without the need for violence or summoning a God."

He stared at the two of them blankly. A distant rumble rocked the room. "Oh, for fuck's sake. What now?"

"Prob'ly my friends," Romy answered. "They would be dumb enough to try and rescue us. They're also just powerful enough to succeed."

He gritted his teeth. "Fine… just… fine. They'll be taken care of in due time. The ritual won't take long anyway."

He walked to the door of the cell and pounded upon it loudly. When it opened David appeared, looking even more feeble and pathetic than he did when Romy last saw him but a couple hours ago.

"David, take them to the altar. We begin immediately."

"But the others are-"

"The others will be unnecessary after I've ripped the Demiurge out of Romy's body. Now grab them and take them to the altar. I must prepare myself."

David nodded. "Yes, sir."

"Wait!" Romy called out, stopping the master mage in his tracks.

"What now???"

"Me and Guy, did you plan that?"

"Did I plan what?"

This was all the answer they needed. "Never mind."

"Never mind what?"

After a period of awkward silence, Guy decided to cut through it like a chainsaw. "We're involved."

Another awkward silence, which Tooth cut. "Well... that's a strange coincidence, I guess."

"Mages don't believe in coincidences, Toothy," Romy says. "Both of your targets ended up in bed together. You don't find that a bit too chaotic?"

"It's definitely strange, and I will gladly ponder upon it after the two of you are dead and I am a walking God on Earth."

And with that Tooth left.

David walked to the still constricted Guy and Romy and activated his periwinkle blue hue. *"Îndepărtaţi legăturile lor. Ridică-te şi urmează."*

The two began to levitate. David walked out of the room, and they floated along behind him.

Despite being unable to move, they could still talk. "David, please. You know this is wrong."

"I know..."

"Then why do it?" Guy asked.

"Because I don't know what else to do. They're my family. Would either of you know what that feels like?"

Romy's heart hurt again. They thought of all the times David would try to defend them, growing up, only to get burned or lashed by Daciana. They watched helplessly as a child as David went from a kind, loving soul to the coward leading them to their death. They had so many questions.

"How long have you known?" They asked.

"About the Demiurge? Ever since you were born."

"You were barely five when I was born. Even then?"

"Even then. I could see your soul for what it was – ancient. Everybody else prob'ly could tell, too, on some level. Which is most likely why they treated you like... well, you know. Eventually, all they could see in you was the garbage they wanted to see. But I never stopped seein' how special you were."

Romy thought deeply about it, and something came to them. "You've seen it before though, right? Like, in person?"

"The day you quit the Coven, the day you left, Daciana sliced your hands off. And then the staff burst out of you, flooded the world around us with the most brilliant light. Your Hue became the sun, the moon, the stars. In an instant, your hands were healed, and you knocked her unconscious with a simple wave. And then you just looked at me."

"Did I say anything?"

"You told me to close my eyes."

"And what did you see?"

"I saw thousands of years' worth of soul residin' within you. I grabbed Daciana and took her back to her room. The staff went back inside you and then you just walked back to your car like nothin' happened."

"One last question."

"What?"

"Where's Grigori?"

"He is safe at home, completely unaware of what's happenin' here. And, I think, that's probably for the best. For what it's worth, despite Tooth's persistence Daciana refused to allow him to be involved."

"Thank the Heathen Gods' she has enough kindness for that."

"It wasn't kindness, it was ego. She was scared Grigori's power, like yours, would put him higher on Tooth's list than her."

"Romy," Guy started. "I normally don't use this kind of language when referring to a woman, but your sister's a bitch."

"Tell me something I don't know."

David blinked. "Romy? I do wonder why you chose that name…"

"Chose? Is Romy not your birth name?"

"Romy is my *true* name. My birth name means nothing to me."

"Understood… How are you holding up?"

"With what?" They responded, facetiously. "Oh, you mean finding out that I'm some sort of *chosen one*, with a powerful magic wand living inside me that this douchebag is planning on using to destroy the world as we know it?"

"Yeah, that."

"Honestly? Pretty okay, all things considered. This definitely answers some questions I've had my entire life. And the whole 'reincarnation' thing pretty much solves every mystery I've ever had about who I am as a person."

Guy was unconvinced. "Are you sure you're not repressing some deeper-seated issues?"

"Guy?"

"Yes?"

"Probably, but maybe let me stay deluded long enough not to have a mental breakdown?"

"Heard, I will chill on the pre-apocalyptic therapy. But afterwards, I am finding you a good therapist."

"I live with one, and I fucked a pretty great one last night."

"A *damn* great one, you mean."

Another explosion rocked the underground prison hallway their captors had built. Dirt began to fall on their heads as David guided them towards the altar room. A great, glowing pentagram was carved into the stone ground, imbued with the magic of every mage in Tooth's employ. At its center was the picture of a goat-headed demon-man etched in blood. Tooth appeared, dressed in a blood red hooded cloak, his hands drenched in what had to have been the same blood used to make the sigil. His face was painted with a demonic visage.

"Let us begin."

Romy sighed. "Well, fuck."

"Romy?"

"Yeah?"

"Remember what I said before? About being glad I met you?"

"You wanna take it back?"

"No. I want you to know I meant it. One hundred percent."

Romy wanted to cry. "Me too, Guy. Me too."

16

The Fight of/for Your Life

"Take out the empath!" Were the first words out of Daciana's mouth.

One of the many ebony-haired, pale-skinned witches activated her aquamarine-colored Hue and clapped her hands. Her magic amplified the resulting sound until it became a massive sonic attack directed at Alfie. Deafened and disoriented, he fell to the ground.

"Whelp," Ianto said, with the urgency of the most cowardly rodent. "That would be my cue." In a flash, he transformed into a vampire bat, releasing himself from his icy restraints and flying away through the nearest upward pipe.

"Saw that coming," Kass said under her breath.

In an instant, both she and Nico had analyzed the situation. Nearly a dozen battle-ready necromancers versus the two of them. Their empath, the ace up their sleeve, had been taken out of play. They were vastly outnumbered and outgunned. However, both had already fought some combination of this group before, which must have been a massive drain on their power. So, they were confident this battle would go one of two ways: total victory, or they would die taking at least half of the zombie-making mages down with them.

"Kill them," Daciana commanded.

Before any of them could try, Nico summoned the sewer water to his side and whipped it at two of their opponents – the witch responsible for taking out Alfie, and the warlock standing beside her. Lassoing their hands, he threw them against the tunnel wall before freezing them into place.

Kass lunged at the warlock she recognized from before who could weaponize his own blood, punching him in the side of the head with at least half of her strength. Enough to knock him out but not enough to twist his head around in its place.

In the corner of her eye, she recognized the vomit witch and quickly threw a roundhouse kick. However, she miscalculated where the kick would land and hit her in the shoulder as opposed to her head. She had to stay focused but was finding it incredulously difficult. She was exhausted and running out of calories to keep herself energized.

'If the world doesn't end tonight,' she thought to herself. 'Burgers. Fries. Food. All the food.'

Nico summoned more water and aimed for Daciana and Raf, both watching anxiously. A witch and a warlock got in the way before he could make contact. Nico thought quickly and maneuvered the water around them to grab his intended target.

Daciana responded instinctively and unleashed a wave of fire that turned the water into steam. She then threw two fireballs, aimed directly at the frozen mages attached to the wall.

"Get your heads in the game, you sad bitches," she yelled as the ice melted away.

One of the witches protecting Daciana and Raf activated a moon silver Hue and summoned what appeared to be several duplicates of herself. Charging at Kass and Nico, they were quickly dispatched by claws and water whips. But when they made contact, the duplicates burst into a cloud of silvery smoke.

"Illusions," Nico pointed out.

"Caught that." Kass attempted to hit another, but it dodged her strike and hit her back with a weak punch to the jaw. "Heads up — they can hurt us."

"Hard Illusions, great." Unlike Kass, Nico's annoyance and anger was the perfect fuel to keep him going.

"How about you let me handle the mages while you heal Alfie?"

"Agreed." Nico went to go help Alfie but was halted by a wall of sewer-dwelling bugs. He repelled in disgust. "What is this?"

"Yeah, these guys do not have the most family-friendly powers. Watch out for the barf girl, by the way."

"Barf girl???"

Seemingly from nowhere, a barf golem appeared and attempted to strike Nico. Acting reflexively while also fighting the urge to vomit himself, he hurled a wave of water, instantly dissolving the grotesque beast. Finding the witch who conjured it, enveloped in an orange Hue, he struck at her with a floating fist made of dirty ice. The impact forced her back into the wall behind her.

A nearby boom signaled an incoming fire which Nico expertly dodged. Daciana's attack, intended for him, hit the wall of bugs instead, creating a hole through which he could pass. Finally reaching Alfie he activated his ice blue Hue and started performing a healing spell. "*Curare.*"

The extraterrestrial empath quickly awoke and began a powerful mental assault on all the nearby mages. Eradicating the ability to conjure their Hues, the playing field was tipped towards Nico and Kass.

"Fuck," was all Daciana could say.

Undiscouraged, the blood-conjuring mage grabbed a nearby fallen pipe and ran towards Alfie. He was stopped, however, by the quick entry of Ianto into the battle zone. Grabbing him by the neck, he pulled him straight into his jowls and began feasting. The warlock, unable to escape, could do nothing as his blood was sucked from his body in a matter of seconds. The others merely looked on in shock.

Finished, Ianto dropped the drained body, made eye contact with his brother and said, "Do not read into this. I was just very hungry."

Alfie did not want to believe him but had no choice. "Understood."

The exchange had the unfortunate side effect of drawing Alfie's attention away from the mages and Daciana threw a fireball at Ianto which he only just barely dodged. Being one of a Vampire's few methods of death, he had learned to avoid fire with a fair proficiency.

A powerful scream filled the tunnel and deafened the lot. The sound manipulating witch had returned. Alfie turned his mental attention towards the witch and removed her aquamarine Hue.

"Take a nap," he instructed her. And with that, she fell asleep standing up. Alfie gently laid her down onto the ground. "Sweet dreams."

"Or not," Ianto said as he moved towards her.

"No eating the unarmed prisoners."

"You are not the boss of me."

Kass, meanwhile, was still fighting her illusory opponents. Alfie turned his attention to the witch producing the illusions and turned off her Hue. Acting quickly, Kass pounced on her and slashed her face, leaving what was certain to be a permanent scar and keep her in pain long enough for her Focus to no longer be a problem.

The tunnel quickly filled with thick black smoke. Thankfully, Alfie had his ESP to guide him while both Ianto and Kass could see ever so perfectly in the dark. The witch producing the smoke never stood a chance against the combined force of Alfie's psychic power and the combination of Ianto and Kass's punches. Both her mind and her face were beaten to a pulp.

Only two warlocks stood to protect Daciana and Raf, and they were both shaking in their boots.

"Just leave," Daciana said. "It's quite clear that the lot of you are useless. Go help Tooth prepare. We'll handle this ourselves."

"But Daciana," One of her followers said, obviously eager to issue a warning.

"Just go," she said with burning, violet eyes. With that, they retreated.

The quartet allowed the two to escape, assured they would be able to capture them later. Daciana and Raf approached them with cautious confidence.

"Be careful," Kass said. "The boy is a mimic."

"Who are you calling 'boy,' beast?"

"You, duh."

"Leave him to me," Nico said. "Get Daciana out of here."

Alfie reached out with his mind and produced a disorienting psychic attack that left Daciana confused enough for Kass to leap at her and toss her into the room beyond the great door. This left Nico standing between Alfie and Raf. Ianto had, once again, disappeared.

"Vampires can be so fickle, can't they?" Raf said, jeeringly.

Alfie knew better. "He knew that you mimicking his power would be a disastrous turn of events."

Raf smiled a villain's smile. "Of course, why else would a Vampire run away? Really the only power I need is yours, my cute little empath." He activated his bright emerald Hue and his body quickly changed to become a near lookalike to Alfie. Using Alfie's powers against Nico, he shut down any chance of the aquamancer using his Hue. "How are you feeling?"

Alfie could not help himself and channeled his ally's emotions. "Incredibly confident and fully aware that you have absolutely no idea what you are dealing with."

Raf's face contorted with confusion. "What?" But then he used his newfound empathy to read Nico further. "Oh…"

Before he could say another word, the water around his feet quickly froze, trapping him in place before Nico sprayed him with a massive geyser of sewer water, throwing him backwards. He quickly recovered, though, and looked at his opponent with astonishment.

"Well, that was… unexpected to say the least. But it'll have to be a mystery I solve after I use your own power against you."

Nico wore a face of determined excitement. "Go right ahead."

Raf, undeterred by Nico's confidence, activated his Hue and proceeded to mirror Nico's very essence. However, something deep within Nico, down to the very core of both his soul and his genes did not sit well with the mimic. His skin turned a pale, translucent white as his chest tightened and his lungs began to lose the ability to search for air.

He gasped and gasped and looked at Nico with horror. "What… are… you???" Before falling unconscious.

"A freak," was Nico's instinctual response. He turned to Alfie, satisfied with his work. "Let's go."

After hurling Daciana into the next room, Kass spread her powerful wingspan and flew after her. Daciana activated her violet Hue and began throwing weak fireballs only to have every one deflected by a simple flap of her wings.

"Starting to get frustrated?" Kass taunted. "Just so I know, is frustration your Focus? If not, then maybe you should take a time out to get your shit together."

Unfortunately for Daciana, she did not have much power, Focus, or energy left. And running on fumes does not an epic battle make. Kass was disorienting Daciana with every flap of her wings, making her incapable of getting in a solid shot. She continued waving as she steadily approached the witch. The battle mage soon fell against the might of the Sphinx and decided to use the last weapon she had left. Her mouth.

"That's it, c'mon you beast!"

"Excuse me?" Kass asked with a raised eyebrow.

"C'mon. Show me that you're an animal. Prove to me that you're nothing more than a monster. Strike me down!"

Daciana was hoping Kass was stupid enough to fall for reverse psychiatry.

She was not.

"Okay!" She delivered a powerful kick to Daciana's chin, knocking her out. "That was disappointing. I hope your master puts up a better fight." Nico and Alfie ran to her side as soon as the fight was over, but the Vampire was nowhere to be found. "Let me guess, Ianto ran?"

"Flew," Alfie corrected her.

"Whatever. Let's just go."

They continued into the great cavern created by the mages, deep towards their altar room made from the remains of a great war shelter. There, they found a man garbed in blood red robes, radiating with a powerful, matching blood red Hue, standing before both Guy and Romy – both clearly in great pain – as a whirlwind of magic surrounded them all. The two surviving mages and a third Alfie recognized as David flanked them. They spied on the trio but did nothing to stop their approach.

"You're too late," David said in the kind of defeated tone one would not expect from a victorious villain. He heaved a heavy, deep, guilt-ridden sigh as he repeated himself. "You're too late…"

Sensing the danger they were in, Romy instinctively summoned the staff buried deep within their soul. The Demiurge that Tooth so desperately desired. He quickly grabbed it.

"Romy!" Kass called out.

Hearing the call, and knowing action was required before they interrupted his extremely sensitive ritual, he slammed the staff into the ground and summoned a horde of zombies from the earth. The undead soldiers grabbed at the three and held them back. Even Alfie was incapable of focusing long enough to disrupt Tooth's magic. Undeterred, he continued on with his demonic rite.

"*Magne deus inferni, princeps daemon Abaddon, te voco. Vocem meam audi et hoc vas ut tuum sume. Esto mihi dux et esto dominus meus in plano isto mortali. Incarnari et caro esse. Magnus inferni deus, princeps daemon Abaddon, te voco. Videte! Videte!*"

As he finished, the very foundation of space and time began to rupture. The ground beneath buckled as a great tear began to form in the air before them. A great collection of devilish, red eyes spied through the hole as a hellish heat filled the room. Clawed hands that were made of pure shadows with veins of red lightning pulsating through them reached out and began to grab at the fissure, tearing it open even further before making its way into the world.

"*Lord Abaddon!*" Tooth called out as he gestured to Guy. "*Take of this vessel before you and be flesh!*"

17

Face Down

It was a perfectly lovely Colorado night. A brisk fall evening. The wind was whistling through the trees. The stars were winking at the happy and smiling family of three driving home together after a night of music.

"Mijo, you did so good," the mom, Gabriela, said from the passenger seat to her seventeen-year-old son, Guy, sitting in the back.

"Thank you, mamá," Guy said back.

"You and that solo. You and that sax!" She mimed playing the saxophone while doing her best to imitate the noise. "Fantástico. Muy magnífico. Bravo! Bravo!"

"Gracias, gracias, I have no time for autographs."

"Tonight, Sterling Music Hall," his father, Gus, added, "tomorrow, the Grammy's!"

Gabriela lightly slapped his arm. "Let's not be crazy."

Gus cleared his throat and his face immediately fell. "Sorry."

Guy could sense the tension and turned his face to the road. At this point in his life, he was used to his parents having strange exchanges whenever the topic of his future came up.

"Speaking of tomorrow," Guy started, taking a deep breath for courage. "We should probably start talking about college soon, since I graduate in, like, ten seconds."

"Ay, mijo, you're so melodramatic. Calm down."

"Okay, but still, I am graduating in a few months, and I haven't picked a college yet. We should talk about where I'm going."

"Oh, Guy, we already know where you're going."

"We do?" Gus asked.

She nudged him. "Yes, we do, mi amor."

"Ah, yeah, I guess we do."

"You'll be going to the University of Colorado."

"I don't remember having that conversation, whatsoever."

"That's because you were not there for it."

Guy rolled his eyes. "Mamá, pleeeeease."

"Pleeeeease what, mijo?"

"You cannot be having important conversations about my future without me. There's, like, a whole mess of factors that I'd like to be clued in on before I decide which school I'm going to."

"Before *you* decide?" She kept prodding. "On your own? Solo?"

"Yes, mom. When *I* decide. I'm the one going to college, not you."

"Yes, but we are the ones paying for you to go to college. And since we are paying, we have the final say. And the final say is: you are going to the University of Colorado."

"Okay, why?" He had to ask.

Gabriela was caught off guard. "Um… because…"

"Yes?"

She lightly hit Gus's shoulder. "Ay, I'm tired of talking. You tell him."

A long, pregnant pause refused to give birth between the two as Gus looked at her with a face that said, "why are you bringing me into this?" She shot back a look that said, "why aren't you getting me out of this?"

He cleared his throat. "Well… son… it has a great music program."

"Not compared to some other schools on the west coast. Like the University of California, which, I should remind both of you, is your alma mater. So, I would hope you have a high regard for it."

"Yes, but just because we went there doesn't mean you have to."

"Yes, and, using that logic, just because you tell me I should go to the University of Colorado does not mean that I will."

"You are not going to school in California," Gabriela said with great authority. "No. I forbid it."

Guy's mouth slacked agape. "You *forbid* it? Mom, that is remarkably not okay."

"How long is this drive home, amirite?" Gus chuckled with the strength of a weak tea. His wife and son looked at him like he had just started speaking gibberish. "Gab, maybe we should just-"

"No, no, there is no discussion. You are going to the University of Colorado. I am putting my foot down."

"Mamá, why are you like this?"

She turned back to him. "Niñito, no me pongas a prueba. Tuvimos una noche maravillosa. Hiciste un trabajo maravilloso. Eres talentoso, eres guapo, tienes padres increíblemente solidarios-"

Gus sighed. "This is fun for me."

"Oh, sí, sí, super solidario. Ni siquiera me dejarás elegir a qué universidad puedo ir. Ustedes son control freaks."

"Control freaks?! Ooooh, Gus, you better pull over. I'm about to roast your son like a chicken."

A flash of lightning. A roll of thunder. Rain started pouring on the small sedan.

"Oh, just fantastic," Gus said to himself as he turned on the windshield wipers.

"What am I doing wrong, exactly?" He asked.

"For one thing, your accent is atrocious. You roll your r's like your tongue is made of paper. And two, your attitude."

"My attitude? *My* attitude?"

Her lawyer started showing. "Yes, *your* attitude. Here you are, a smart, gifted young man with so much going for him. Two parents who are still married. Willing to pay for your college so you can go to school and make your music and sing your songs without the specter of debt hanging over your head. And yet, you must pick at it. And pick at it, pick at it, pick at it till it's just bones. And you know who wants to eat bones? Nobody. You are trying so hard to make a bad thing out of a good thing, you are not appreciating all that we have given you."

"Mamá, I appreciate everything you've given me. I do! But I want to go where I want to go. Not where you want to go. I love you both so much, but you have to let me breathe and go my own way."

"Gabriela," Gus was about to start until she gave him a look. "Never mind. I am not a part of this."

"Guy, you have to-"

A flash of red lightning. The family screamed as they lost control of the car and flew off the road. It spun and tumbled and became crushed under its own weight as it fell down the hill.

"Mom? Dad?"

18

Demon Daze

Tooth felt victorious. Years of scheming and planning had finally come to fruition as he held the Demiurge in one hand and imminent triumph in the other.

However, the Prince of Hell was clearly unsatisfied with the vessel he was being presented with. *"You cannot be serious,"* the demon said in a voice that chilled every bone in the room. Nails on a chalkboard.

"By the Gods…" Nico whispered as a rotted arm kept him from running to his ex and his ex's rebound's rescue.

Alfie remained too stunned to move, overwhelmed by the intense emotions rushing through the room. Only Kass struggled against her zombie captors, but any time she cut one down, another would instantly rise to take its place. The combined power of the staff and the Demon God was fueling the summoning sigil beyond its limit.

Confused, Tooth attempted to regain control of the situation. "My Lord, Abaddon, what-"

"You think me a fool, you false immortal? You present me a pitiful boon — a revenant corpse — and expect me to accept with blind gratuity?"

"My lord?"

The Devil God forced himself through the small tear in the universe. Manifesting in the world for the first time in eons, he took a form that could only be described with words that cannot be allowed to exist. Violent thoughts made flesh. Murderous rage, crippling fear, and shattering grief creating a vacuum that brutally sucked the hope, love, and kindness from the room. Even Kass, with all her zeal and tenacity, fell to her knees and cried at his visage. Alfie's nose began bleeding a gross, florescent pink as his eyes rolled back into his head. Nico vomited what little remained in his stomach. David and his fellow necromancers fell face first to the floor, unconscious from the sheer trauma of just looking at him.

The only ones who remained standing were the arrogantly confident Tooth, and Romy. A soul too old to be frightened of a demon.

The demon lord spoke with a voice like a knife to an innocent child's throat. *"You bear a stolen weapon. A gift from my treacherous brethren to the riotous virus of humanity. A stolen weapon you intend to use to rob me of my power to replace your weak and tattered magic with my endlessness. You are a fool. I allowed you to invoke my power for as long as you have with full intent to bring me to this very moment in time and space. With the knowledge that you would summon me and think to rob me of my greatness. But how could one bound to this mortal world ever truly be capable of grasping infinity?"*

Tooth, never deterred, held up the staff. "Lord Abaddon, I bind you-"

*"You will bind nothing but your tongue, death conjurer. "*With a slight wave of his wicked hand, he released a draining, crushing rush of pure despair. A blanket of darkness that seeped into Tooth's every pore. Infecting him like a disease.

He finally fell to his knees, dropping the Demiurge to the ground where it flew back to Romy and disappeared within them. They felt a sudden rush of energy through their body, mind, and soul.

"I would never allow myself to be anchored to necrotic flesh, nor manipulated by an ignorant, vain necromancer, tainted by his own conceit. " The demon God turned his attention to the young mage. *"You, however... "* His venom eyes looked deep into an unblinking Romy's. *"You are a vessel I find myself very interested in. "*

"Suck a dick and die, you trash God."

"So feisty. I shall enjoy weaponizing your body and using it to bend this world to my every whim."

"As if." Romy defiantly stood against the Demon and raised their hands. However, to their shock, they could not activate their Hue. "Oh no."

"You think to use your base magic against a being who supplies you with that very gift? How adorable." He stretched out his vile hand and began to radiate a cancerous energy. *"Perhaps I should find a different receptacle to embody my essence in this world."* He released a blast of dark force that pierced through Romy's heart and plunged them into a dark void.

"NO!" They heard Kass scream as they faded into nothingness.

19

Give Up the Ghost

They were gone. They were surrounded by oblivion. A cold emptiness. They were sure they were dead.

They could hear echoes of the past. All the people they had let down.

Kass. "You're fabulous. You know that right?"

Nico. "I will always love you. No matter what."

Alfie. "Feelings of isolation, rejection, and depression. You will recover from this. It will be okay."

Grigori, their little brother. "I hate it here! Please! Take me with you!"

Bună. "As long as you know you are great, you will be greater."

Guy. "Everywhere I go, I feel you."

Themself. "Well... I guess this is goodbye, cruel adventure game."

"Don't be silly, my child," a voice like a sweet, familiar lullaby, aged yet delicate, said softly to them through the darkness. "You're not dead. That's impossible."

"What? Who is that? Where are you? What do you mean?"

From literally nowhere, the nothingness was replaced by verdant, green fields. A small house on a prairie surrounded by lush apple trees. A purple sky as twilight set in. A small table and two chairs on the porch. A kettle with freshly hot tea and matching, ornamental teacups. An old woman in a simple black dress and a witch's hat who looked so familiar it was scary.

"Wait… Bună?" They asked.

"No, but close enough. Had I been alive the same time as you, you may have called me your Grand-bună."

"Grand-bună? Wait…" They took a better look at her. "Are you Minadora Ardelean?"

"Yes and no." She took a sip and recoiled. "Ugh, this tea is terrible. Who taught you how to brew?"

"I didn't make it."

She eyed them suspiciously. "It's not apropos to lie to your guests dear."

"It's not very 'apropos' to accuse someone of lying when they've just died."

She rolled her eyes. "Darling, do you not understand what's going on here?"

"Truly, grand-bună, I do not. Last I checked, I was getting straight murdered by Abaddon, Prince of Hell, and plunged into infinite darkness. Now I'm here in this gorgeous glade, and while I'm not complaining I'm certainly not conscious of what the fuck is going on. I mean, am I in the Aether? Is this the spirit world? Is this heaven? Cuz it sure as hell don't feel like it. It feels way too nice and inviting and… concrete to be something as abstract as the afterlife. And, quite frankly, I'm incredibly finished with a bunch of ancient mages – no offense – condescending to me. Now if you have the power to enlighten me, please do, cuz I'm coming up with butt-kiss."

"The correct term is 'bubkes', darling."

"I know what the correct term is, granny."

She sighed warmly and smiled at them. "This is your soul's palace, my love. Everything here is a figment of your innermost yearnings. The grand beauty and simple joys you long for. A beautiful sunset in the old country. A cup of tea with a kind stranger. But truly, I am not a stranger. Am I?"

They looked at her sideways. "Not really, no. I mean – you died before I was even born so I only know you from your pictures and the spells you left behind. But, I guess, I always identified with you. Coming to a new world, strange and unfamiliar. Starting a coven all on your own with nothing but your children and a grimoire."

"And a staff that no one remembers."

Romy's eyes widened. "Grand-bună, did you wield the Demiurge before me?"

"I was you before you were you."

"Okay..."

"Truly, I was beginning to worry that you would never invoke us but, it appears, it had to wait until you were ready. Unfortunately, it took almost dying for you to get there. For me, it was giving birth for the first time. Of course, I was fourteen so – obviously – there was some stress involved."

"Valid. But how did we get here?"

"You brought us here. Through sheer force of will."

"Wow... okay... good on me, I guess."

"Would you rather be somewhere else? Perhaps, at home, with a very special someone?"

The green pastures suddenly transformed into Romy's bedroom. They watched as they saw a vision of themselves naked in bed with Guy. The two were holding each other close.

"Is this it?" Guy asked, emanating an aura that was part afterglow and part anxiety. "Is this what endgame feels like?"

"What do you mean?" Romy responded in a relaxed tone.

"I mean, is this what happens after the end of the movie? Do we finally get to have the happily ever after we've always dreamed of? I'm not going to lie, for a long time, I thought we were never going to make it. I thought I was going to die or you were going to die or both. But then we made it through. And now, I don't know what is scarier, the threat of death or the reality that now we have a whole future to plan together."

Romy laughed, softly, not at Guy but at the situation. "And here I was thinking that I was the worry wort."

"And I'm supposed to be the therapist in the relation-ship."

"Let's get something straight before we go anywhere with this: you are not my therapist. You are my lover. I support you, I love you, for better or worse, sicker or poorer, all that good stuff. But it's not your job to bear the weight of my emotional problems. I'm here for you, no matter what, but I have no intention of saddling you with my crap."

"But I want you to saddle me with your crap. I want all of you. All the strings attached."

Both Romy and Minadora could see this vision for what it was. It wasn't just some fantasy. It was the future. Not a hopeful illusion but a very real and very powerful divination.

"Okay, this is weird right?"

"Yes, it is, even for us," she said.

"How do I make it go away?"

"I told you. You will it. You wanted peace. You wanted help and you brought us here. You brought me here to help. So, bring us somewhere else. Please, before I get an eyeful."

Romy closed their ethereal eyes and concentrated. When they opened them again, they were back in the fields. Hundreds of magenta butterflies were flittering about.

"Whoa."

"Yes, I know. It's truly a spectacle to enter a soul palace for the first time. By the by, shall we discuss how to best help you?"

"How can you help me? I'm dead."

"Weren't you listening, earlier, when I said you *can't die?*"

"I can't die?"

"Well, I guess a better turn of phrase would be 'won't die.' At least not at the hands of an aether-being."

"What do you mean?"

"Our very existence is meant to keep the Gods at bay, Romy. The Demiurge, being one of the four weapons used to strike them down and exile them. If the Gods could so easily destroy us, then what is the point? So long as the Demiurge is attached to our soul, it can never be extinguished by someone so puny as a Hell God." She rolled her eyes. "Please."

"I'm sorry, how many hell Gods did you fight in your lifetime?"

"Plenty. Our Master Tooth out there is not the first, nor will he be the last, to ever attempt a summoning of this nature. Each one of your past incarnations has fought at least one. I believe the average is around three, or two-and-a-half. I'm not sure, it's been sometime since we could commune in such a fashion."

"Commune?"

"We're here to help you, darling. Outside this palace of yours is the first real fight of your life. And it's plain that you need to realize who you truly are. And you need all the help you can get to make that happen. Many incarnations ago, our brave but admittedly short-sighted sister Beatrix Bishop cast the Demiurge from the memories and minds of those who would abuse it."

"So... everybody?"

"Yes, everybody. Now shut up and let me talk."

"By the Heathen Gods, fine. But could you keep it to the cliff's notes?"

"No. Unfortunately, Beatrix's spell had the unforeseen consequence of causing even the bearers of the Demiurge to forget its existence until the day we come into our power."

"But – and stop me if I'm wrong – I think I've used the staff before. Why am I only just now 'coming into my power?'"

She scoffed. "Those trite little battles were nothing compared to Abaddon. He may be a lowly Prince of Darkness but he's a far flight from a poltergeist. To use your turn of phrase: like, come on."

"So, I've just been waiting for this day my entire life?"

"Pretty much, darling. You see, it's not a matter of just using the staff. It's embracing the magic of your ancient soul. It's embracing yourself. It's truly understanding your place in the world and who you are, who you're meant to be, and who you have been. We're here to welcome you. And we're so happy to have you."

"We?"

"Of course, we. Look out into the world you've created for yourself."

They gazed upon the beautiful landscape they painted on the canvas of their heart. From the imaginary earth sprouted hundreds of beautiful magenta flowers. Within each lay a soul, or, indeed, a different piece of the puzzle that was Romy's soul. Each blossomed, one by one, and with every one came what felt like an embrace to Romy. A powerful, loving embrace.

"Now, my dear, don't you think it's about time you left? Last I checked, you had a *few* handsome suitors out in the real world you need to save."

They looked out into the twilight horizon, but the sun wasn't setting. It was rising.

The slowly dying stars edged closer to them as they floated in mid-air. And then they weren't stars. They were familiar faces they had never seen before. Hands outstretched to lift them up.

A wizened wizard dressed in medieval robes using the staff to battle a sea of dragons.

A man from the Tupi Tribe using the staff to banish a centipede demon.

A woman with one arm from Ancient Alexandria fighting a terrible war with only the staff and her owl familiar by her side.

A female knight with short, boyish hair, holding the staff in one hand and a brilliant sword in another as she casts down the demon queen, Lilith.

A two-spirit shaman using the staff to heal an entire tribe of Chippewa natives after a grueling battle with the invading colonists.

A young Japanese girl, wearing a beautiful, magenta, silk yukata using the staff to kill an entire horde of demon women attempting to rip open the Aether.

A Xhosa chieftain using the staff to make an entire island invisible to protect its inhabitants from slavers.

A Spanish noble with a brilliant mustache using the staff to take his lover on a walk on the face of the moon.

Minadora using the staff to stop a world-ending comet from hitting the earth.

Beatrix Bishop, the very battle mage who began this adventure ages before Romy was born, using the staff to end the Witch War before erasing the world's knowledge of its existence. Sundering it into nothing more than a myth for mage storybooks.

The hundreds of stars surrounded them in their brilliant light and swept them upwards until they reached the end of the sunlight filled vortex they once felt completely lost in. And then they saw it: the staff, waiting for them to take control.

20

Alive & Kicking

They emerged from the void Abaddon had cursed them into and stared the beast down in his now danger-less eyes. In fact, he appeared to almost be trembling at the sight of their brilliant Hue, radiating goodness and light to combat the pure hate emanating from the pitiable creature.

"You wielders truly do not die so easily, I see."

Throwing themself to the ground, they slammed down the staff and created a powerful wave of magenta light. In a shocking instant, the summoning sigil was erased and every zombie in the room – and in all of Boston –returned to dust and blood and bone. The red sky opened up to reveal a brilliant full moon, on a half-moon night.

The sheer might of this attack sent Abaddon flying backwards. Regaining his footing, he summoned a sea of razor blades made of pure terror and threw them at the still freshly resurrected Romy.

Without flinching, they summoned music played not on instruments but with the sheer concept of joy and love. Drowning out the demon's attack, they gazed at him with wide, alert eyes.

"You will not befall us this easily, devil." Their voice was not their own, but a chorus of thousands of years of magic come to claim this battle a victory. Every word they spoke was a spell. Every syllable, a nail in Abaddon's coffin.

"You have come into your own, staff-bearer, but I am far more powerf-"

They interrupted him. *"Oh, shut up. This ends one way. And one way only."*

The demon conjured a hail of burning nightmares. They countered with a bubble made of the purest light. A light that made every living being in the room giggle. Including Abaddon, who recoiled in disgust.

He roared. *"I will not be undone by such a creature! I am the undoing!"*

He put all of his black bile soul into a blast of dark lightning, only to have it swatted away as if it were a hair caught in Romy's eye.

"We all have high opinions of ourselves, until we meet someone higher."

"Enough of these tricks!" He ran at them.

"Would you prefer a treat, my little bitch?"

He grasped at the staff. **"I want you, and this staff, to die!"**

"It sucks when we can't get what we want, doesn't it?"

The staff became so cold in his hands, it burned. He screamed like a child as he fell backwards, no longer capable of keeping himself aloft. From the earth around him, Abaddon was struck with glowing hands that chained him to the ground. With all their magical might, they held him down and prepared for the final blow. Throwing themselves at the cretin, they activated the true power of the Demiurge and struck at the very core of his being. Catching his heart in the apex of the staff, they pulled it into the palm of their hands and felt his life beating away.

"Demon God, Abaddon. Go back to the Hell that is your kingdom, and your prison. And tell your friends… I'm waiting." And with those words, they crushed the heart and watched as the beast evaporated into small magenta butterflies that flew into the tear in the aether. Abaddon was no more.

Lifting the staff once again, they sewed the rip back together. Removing the possibility of any others following in the Demon God's footing.

Just then, Daciana and her horde appeared. Looking at the devastation before them, they were terrified.

"What did you do?!" She demanded an explanation with a fearful voice.

Ignoring her, they turned their attention to the fallen Henry Tooth. They looked at him with pity as he cried on his knees before their very sight. He looked up at them with teary eyes.

"I think we can both agree, it's time for you to rest."

And with a Hue-covered kiss to his forehead, they brought Tooth's long overdue end. He disappeared into a cloud of blood red dust with what sounded like a happy sigh of relief.

Daciana began to cry. "NOOOOOOO!"

Romy simply turned to face her and her kin with blazing eyes. *"And now for you."* Slamming the staff to the ground once again, they conjured nine magenta hands to grab at the surviving, traitorous Ardeleans and dragged them all towards themself.

"You have forsaken the gift of magic, brought shame to your family name, and played party to a plot that sacrificed countless souls while debasing the very foundation of necromancy to your own selfish ends. For that, I bestow upon you the greatest punishment I can conjure."

"What will you do then?" Daciana asked. "Kill us?"

"We deserve no less," David said, for once not under his breath.

"No, dear sister… something far worse." The Hues of each individual Ardelean activated against their will as Romy turned the staff into a terrifying scythe of pure magical force. Slashing at the group, the witches suddenly felt the world around them grow cold as their Hues dissipated.

"What-" Daciana gasped for air as she felt her connection to the aether burn away from the inside out. "What did you do?!"

"I ripped the magic from your souls. You will never cast again."

"Romy?" Guy said, weakly as the last remaining shreds of Tooth's life force began leaking out of him. "Help…" He fell towards the ground.

Romy caught him with the power of the staff and imbued him with all the ancient magic they could find to remove Tooth's revenant curse from his body. Bringing him back to life – making him truly alive. A feat accomplished as simply as if they were washing their hands.

With clear eyes, he looked at them and gasped. His great blue eyes widened, like they were opening for the first time.

"Oh my God… Oh my God! Romy!" He stood up and prepared to run to them only to be intercepted by Kass who tackled the newly empowered mage to the ground.

"ROMY! THAT WAS SO AWESOME! YOU FACED THE DEMON GUY THINGY CREEP AND

THEN HE THREW YOU INTO A BLACK HOLE BUT
THEN YOU FLEW OUT OF IT AND THEN YOU
BLASTED HIM INTO PIECES AND THEN WHOOSH
AND BLAAAAAH AND WWWHAAAAAA AND- and-
and... THAT WAS SOOOOO COOL!"

The others approached cautiously.

"I do not know how necessary this would be to say,
but Kass is full of joy."

"Thank you, Alfie, I can see that." They pulled themself back to their feet with the staff before reabsorbing it back
into their soul. "Are you all okay?"

"More than okay, in my case," Guy said.

Romy looked at them meekly. "I did what I could."

"You did more than enough."

"You took away their magic?" Nico asked, a twinge of
fear in the back of his throat.

"I thought it appropriate, given the circumstances. Do
you not approve?"

"Oh! No! Gladly, I just thought it was cool how easy it
was for you to do."

"Nico is skeptical and worried of reprisals."

"I can sense that, Alfie, thank you."

"If you can sense emotions now, I shall take my leave."

"That was sarcasm, sweetie," Kass said.

"I know, I just thought I would have fun, for a change." He wiped the blood from his nose onto his shirt sleeve. "But, yes, Nico is scared of you now, Romy."

"I understand why," They spoke in a reassuring voice. "But he has no need to be. I would never use the staff on any of you. I love you guys, all of you." They said this while maintaining eye contact with Nico.

Guy saw this and shifted uncomfortably in his place.

"Speaking of the staff," Kass started. "Isn't it about time that we forgot about it? Like, isn't that how this works? You use it, it goes away, and then we forget it all?"

"Yeah, honestly, that whole curse thing needed a little upgrade. So, I thought, why not let you guys be the ones who get to remember it all."

"Why, though?" Guy asked.

"Because I trust you," they said with a smile.

Guy smiled back. Pure sunshine.

The clopping of hooves and the pounding of dozens of soldiers' boots marked the arrival of the MIST agents. Armed to the teeth and ready for battle, Lustre led the charge as she entered the room.

Left with no battle to be fought, she gaped at the besieged altar room before her and demanded an answer. "What happened???"

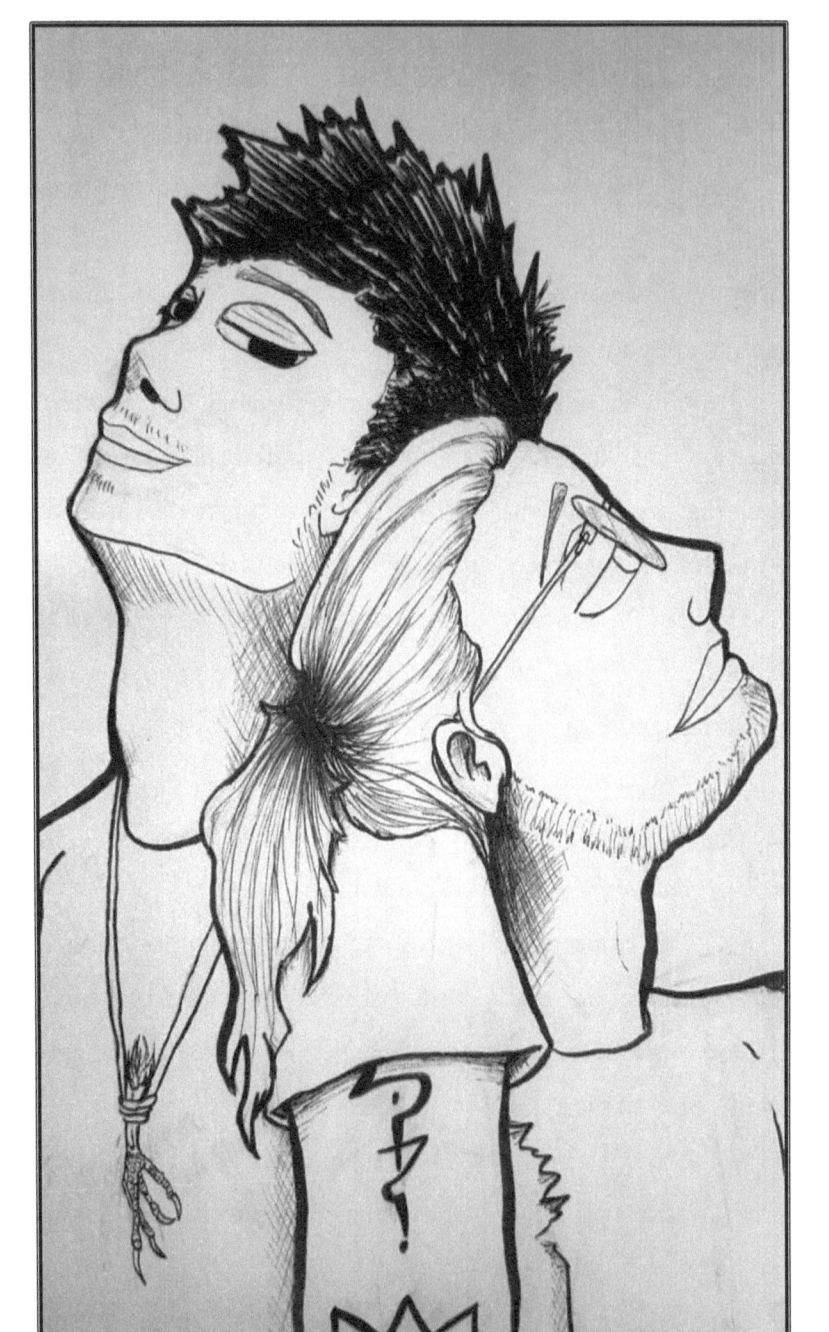

Now You See It

"Crisis and Chaos in the Cradle of Liberty as Boston is plagued by a gross horde of zombies," The Anchorman recited with a puffed chest. "It has been a month since the City on the Hill went black and we are only now just receiving reports from Boston MIST as to what really went down in Beantown."

"Can this guy be any more pompous?" Kass asked the room from her position mere inches away from the television resting on the floor of her living room.

In the time since "Z-Day," Romy and their friends had managed to keep a relatively low profile despite being at the center of everything. Nobody asked them any hard questions, all they cared about was that the danger was over and the witches responsible were either dead or depowered. The room-mates' "cataclysm insurance" allowed them to recover most of the property damaged by the Ardeleans, including replacing the incinerated Nick Jonas with a new cactus, Gus Kenworthy.

"Kass, shhh," Guy said as he threw popcorn at her.

"We go now to Elaina Rodriguez on the scene. Elaina"

"Thank you, Tom. Boston, the Athens of America-" she was interrupted by a sudden fast forwarding.

"Yeah, we don't need to hear this," Kass said only to be bombarded with more popcorn. "It's a recording, you dick sandwiches. You can rewatch it whenever you want."

"Wait!" Guy called out. "Stop! It's Nico's interview! Look, Nic, you're on T.V."

"Oh Gods, I look so pale…"

"You look gorgeous," Kass corrected him. "Now shut up and watch yourself be awkward on camera."

Nico watched himself through his hands. "The important fact is that we've isolated the threat and are allocating proper recovery efforts to focus on… recovery."

"Yes," Miss Rodriguez said, with a professionally courteous tone that barely masked her combined bemusement and amusement. "And what can you say about the perpetrators."

"All we can say on that matter is that the perpetrators were a crew of rogue, malignant and… um… reprobate necromancers who-" Kass paused the recording.

"Did you really just say 'reprobate?'"

"By the Heathen Gods, Kass," Guy said with yet another wad of popcorn.

"Bro, can I just say that while I'm happy you're here – and you're totally welcome into my home anytime – this is still *my home*. And I like my home most when there's no popcorn on the floor." She threw the pillow she kept under her stomach at her newly mortal guest.

Alfie felt the need to interject. "I would like to watch Nico and his performance on the news, please."

"Yeah, whatever," Kass pressed a button, thinking she was resuming the video, only for it to quickly cut ahead to the main anchorman. "Oh, shit, what did I do?"

"You skipped through the whole thing!" Nico exclaimed.

"I'm sorry, I'll go back!" She began punching random buttons on the remote, obviously out of her ken.

"This is why we never had watch parties," He groaned.

Guy checked his watch and sprang off the couch. "It's whatever, guys. I gotta go pick up Romy anyway."

"Is he staying at your place tonight?" Kass asked.

"Kass…" Guy said, gesturing towards Nico.

"Oh, please. As if he doesn't know you two are dating?"

Nico tried breaking the tension with a lie. "It's okay, Guy." Alfie was about to say something, but Nico threw his hand over his mouth. "For real, it's okay. Give Romy my love."

Guy awkwardly eyed the room. "Okay. Bye friends." And with that, he grabbed his jacket and fluttered out the door.

"It is very awkward for you to be around them," Alfie channeled Nico's emotions.

"But we both know that personal growth requires personal sacrifice," Nico countered.

"Yes, but it also requires personal space," Alfie volleyed back.

"Ugh, can you not be so insightful?" Nico asked.

"It is literally all that I am."

Kass pulled their attention back to the television. "Hey, guys, watch."

The anchorman continued talking. "As we speak, *'human rights'* watchdog groups are amassing at the gates of senates and governors' mansions alike, using Boston as an example of the need for greater policing of mages and other 'mystical creatures' all over the country. The Massachusetts governor issued this response to the outpouring of vitriol against mages-"

"Well, fuck," was all Kass could say.

Romy approached the bulletproof glass window and picked up the phone as David, their once upon a time cousin, did the same.

"Hey," they said.

"Hi," he said softly back.

"So..."

"So..."

It was awkward to say the least.

"How's it going in-"

David interrupted them. "Are you gon' tell me why I still have my magic?"

"Straight to the point? Wow, jail really does change people. Also, shhhh. Don't broadcast."

"I'm only in jail cuz I know I deserve to be here – and I couldn't bear to face the coven back home – but I think we both know that I could leave whenever I wanted to. Why did you let me keep my powers?"

"Why wouldn't I? You were as much an innocent pawn as any other victim of Daciana's-"

"Romy, come on."

They sighed. "Okay… so, your power enables you to see things others can't."

"Yes?"

"Including my staff."

"Of course. Is this goin' anywhere anytime soon?"

"Seriously, this is an incredible one-eighty for your character."

"I'm in prison for crimes against humanity. I'm facin' the death sentence. That type of stuff changes a person. Please, Romy, just talk to me."

"I need you to kill me if I ever go rogue," they said with bated breath.

David looked at them like they were speaking gibberish. "What?"

"I'm a ticking time bomb with both hands at eleven."

"Fuck the metaphors and just tell me what's goin' on."

"I've been having dreams, lately. At least, I thought they were dreams. It's only been a couple weeks, but ever since that night with Abaddon and Tooth and everything, I've been seeing things. Visions. Pathways of time and choice and..." They trailed off as their mind was wiped with a daydream of possible ends to the conversation.

David offers a gesture of support and kindness. David refuses to listen and runs away. David uses his magic to escape from prison and kidnaps Romy to hide them away from the rest of the world. David kills Romy on sight.

"Romy, are you okay?" He touched the glass.

"HANDS OFF THE GLASS!" The guard shouted, causing David to recoil.

"I'm seeing the consequences of choices I haven't even made yet. It's hard to explain, but it's like I'm breaking down the very fabric of chaos. Or string theory. Or whatever those guys on Big Bang Theory talk about. I pick up a cup of coffee and I see how that cup of coffee will change my day. I put it down and I see myself go through my day, my life, with or without that coffee. To be or not to be, seeing every action and its path stretch out before me. I've conferred with all of my past incarnations-"

"Past incarnations?"

"Oh, yeah, that's another thing I can do. I can talk to my past lives. It's weird. But helpful."

"Past lives?"

"Yeah."

"You can talk to your past lives now?"

"Yeah, including our great-grandmother."

David's eyes remained as wide as a child's. "Go on."

"Anyway, I was speaking to a couple of my past lives and apparently this is unheard of. I'm doing things that nobody who's ever wielded the staff has done before. And it's getting *worse*. I'm looking back on everything that's happened. All the unexplained coincidences. The only thing that really makes any sense is that I've been manipulating things – I've been manipulating everybody and everything in my life to help bring me to this moment."

"Romy-"

"I know you know what I'm talking about. I've been playing with the strings of fate. Nico. Kass. Alfie. Even Guy. They're all in my life because they *needed* to be in my life. They're not with me because they want to be. I gathered this cast of characters and perfectly arranged everything so that, when the time came, they'd be able to help me save the day. What does this say about the life I've built? About the life I want to lead? Do any of them love me? Could any of them really love me if they knew what I did without even trying to do it?"

"Romy…"

"David, listen. If this magic gets the best of me, if I pull a Daciana and start spam-pressing the renegade button, I need you to help my friends take me down. I trust them, and I trust you."

"But-"

"TIME'S UP!" The guard shouted before pulling David away from the glass.

Romy hung up the phone and waved goodbye. With their magic, without even activating their Hue, they spoke straight to his mind. 'I believe in you.'

Walking outside, they smiled as they saw Guy step out of his little yellow beetle.

"Hey cutie," they called out.

"Hello, my sexy steady." Guy's affectionate, non-binary term for Romy.

"No, you're sexy."

"No, we're *both* sexy."

"I like that answer."

"I like you. Now get in the car, you filthy animal."

"Yes, sir." Romy jumped into the car and got ready for an adventure. "Where you takin' me today?" Romy needed Guy to make the decisions because they could never see him coming. His whimsical randomness kept them guessing. And they needed to guess. They needed random. They had to find a way to stop seeing everything, and Guy was slowly starting to look like the key to all of that.

"I was thinking of a whole lot of watching the sunset and just basking in each other's awesomeness while eating tons of carbs."

"I like that answer."

"I like you." Guy grabbed Romy's hand and kissed it. "For real."

"So," Romy felt like checking in, "how are you holding up? Not being a revenant anymore."

This was the first time they had asked this question since Z-Day. "Gosh, it's like… it's like not being able to taste sugar your entire life, and then suddenly you can. It was wonky, at first. But then I felt this constant warmth. And I realized, it was you. It was your magic deep inside me."

"Hubba hubba," Romy could not help but joke.

"No, for real though. Everywhere I go, I feel you. Whether I wake up with you in my arms or not, your magic is wrapping me up like a blanket. And I love… it."

They were not ready for "I love you's" yet, but Guy wanted to say it so badly. Romy wanted to say it too. But then Romy saw what would happen if they did say it. They saw them going too fast in their relationship and burning out. They saw them being together for the rest of their lives. They saw them being together for literally ever, until the end of time. They saw Guy dying in at least a hundred different ways. They saw themself die, young, in Guy's arms. They also saw Guy wielding a sword and protecting Romy from some unknown villain. They saw a world without magic. They saw a world where magic never existed to begin with. They saw a world populated and ruled, once again, by the villainous Gods. They saw a world without shrimp. They saw a world without birds. They saw a world without humans. They saw a world where extraterrestrials ruled. They saw a world where Romy was never born. They saw a world where Daciana was a good person. They saw a world where David was the owner of the staff. They saw visions

But all of that would have to wait as they tried to focus on the present.

All of that would have to wait as they tried to focus on Guy, and his beautiful, sunshine smile. And their beautiful, sunrise future.

To Be Continued...

Meet the Cast

(In order of appearance)

Romy, the Hedge

Pronouns: They/Them

Place of Birth: The Ardelean Coven Grounds in Georgia

Occupation: Necromancer

Fun Fact: Loves watching British sitcoms

First Language: English & Romanian

Astrological Sign: Aries

Date of Birth: 4/17/1992

Chinese Astrological Sign: Monkey.

Favorite Playlist: Queer Love Songs

Most Repeated Song: Linger by the Cranberries.

Favorite Color: Pink and Black

Favorite Food: Stroganoff

In their spare time, they: Like to read YA novels

Alfie Pugh

Pronouns: He/Him

Place of Birth: Korkorma City on the Continent of Daad (best translation), Planet Nine

Occupation: Clinical Therapist and Empath

Fun Fact: Born on an eclipse of three moons

First Language: English & Welsh

Astrological Sign: N/A

Date of Birth: 1/1/2001 (assigned birthday, not actual)

Chinese Astrological Sign: Snake

Favorite Playlist: None.

Most Repeated Song: None

Favorite Color: Salmon

Favorite Food: Bara Brith

In his spare time, he: Plays video games.

Guy Garrison

Pronouns: He/Him

Place of Birth: Beverly Hills, California

Occupation: Music Therapist

Fun Fact: Has a bachelor's degree in music therapy and a master's in clinical psychiatry

First Language: Spanish & English.

Astrological Sign: Libra

Date of Birth: 10/19/1994

Chinese Astrological Sign: Dog

Favorite Playlist: Best of 80's New Wave.

Favorite Song: Rock Lobster by the B-52's.

Favorite Color: Blue.

Favorite Food: Borscht

In his spare time, he: Plays in a band called The Harmonica Lewinski's and enjoys cooking

Kassandra "Kass" Al-Amin

Pronouns: She/Her

Place of Birth: Cairo, Egypt.

Occupation: MIST Agent

Fun fact: She is Lactose intolerant.

First Language: Arabic and French.

Second Languages (Fluent): English, Spanish, German.

Astrological Sign: Leo (duh)

Date of Birth: July 30th, 1996

Chinese Astrological Sign: Rat

Favorite Playlist: Bad Bitch Shit – best of hot femme rappers

Favorite song: Bitch Better Have My Money by Rihanna

Favorite color: Gold.

Favorite Food: Burger

In her spare time she: Teaches a pole-dancing class.

Nicodemo "Nico" Acquati.

Pronouns: He/Him

Place of Birth: Palermo, Sicily

Occupation: MIST Agent

Fun fact: Vegan.

First Language: Italian & English.

Astrological Sign: Cancer

Date of Birth: July 14th, 1992 (Full Moon)

Chinese Astrological Sign: Monkey

Favorite Playlist: Piano Music for Meditation

Favorite song: Pre-breakup "Breathe Me" by Sia, post-breakup "River" by Joni Mitchell

Favorite color: Sea Green

Favorite Food: Soy Latte

In his spare time, he: Practices his magic as much as possible.

Acknowledgments

This has been a truly wondrous journey. A journey I took with one goal: to write a story about a non-binary person. This book truly is a love letter to all the trans/non-binary people in and out my life.

I should go on to thank my family – Mom, Kirsten, and Brendon. All those nights watching Buffy the Vampire Slayer together truly helped me hone my love for paranormal fantasy and kick ass femme and queer characters. You blessed me with a love of creative arts, and I'll be eternally grateful. Your love and support helped encourage me to become a queer story-teller.

And then there's my chosen family – Chris and Shane. Dalaya and Hunter. Matt. Michael. Garrett. Sadie. Reese. Harold. You amazing people inspired me to write this story and helped me hone my voice and creative process.

Daniel, my steadfast editor and consistent supporter. This book wouldn't exist without you.

Ezra Komo. The artist to end all artists. You are a king among peasants. You came in and did the thing and did it well. I am so blessed to have you as a friend and as an artist.

My Nclusion+ Boys –Anthony, Brandon, Ben, Chris – you keep me on the stage. You keep me blessed. You keep me coined. Where would I be without you guys? Probably burned at the stake.

To my fabulous queens: Artemis Grey. Bella Rose. Bea Jay Enidae. Faye King. Kay Cee Adams. Veronika Versace. Liz Anya. Lorilei. Bennifer Lopez. Muffie Beaverhausen. Remi Dee. Lisa de la Renta. Venus O'Hara. Katherine Feiner. May O'Naise. Luna Steelheart. Drag is magic and you are all amazing witches.

My friends at the Skylark Bookshop. Carrie and Alex. Reading stories in your shop helped make me braver and more sure of myself as an artist, an author, and a friend.

The Dandy Lion staff – Kate, Lynn, Sage, Lex, Paul. This book could sell zero copies but seeing it on your shelf would be priceless.

The fates were kind enough to bring you all into my life. Thank you.

About the Author

Autumn Equinox (they/them) lives in Columbia, Missouri with their cat, Archibald Maguire "Archie" Equinox (he/him) and performs as a drag queen outside of being an author. They are originally from Seattle, Washington.

They love reading stories to children through Drag Storytime, playing Pokémon, and taking long hot bubble baths while eating chocolate cake cuz they are a Queen.

This is Autumn Equinox's second published work. Their first novel, "Project: Wonders," is available for purchase through both Amazon and Barnes & Noble.

Instagram: @autumnequinoxious
Facebook.com/autumnequinoxious
Twitter: @equinoxious

www.ingramcontent.com/pod-product-compliance
Lightning Source LLC
Chambersburg PA
CBHW032206030726
47494CB00020B/634